Olivia Daisy Phillips is the author of the new romance book *Smooth Like Whiskey*. She wanted to make this book relevant and reach out to other women who felt the same as she has done. Writing a book has been a dream of hers ever since she was younger, and now this dream has become a reality. It's definitely a pinch-me moment for Olivia. She plans on writing a lot more books in the future, and cannot wait to start tapping away again. Find out more about her current life on her Instagram page: @oliviadaisyphillips.

I dedicate this book to the girls who have never felt smart enough, pretty enough or thin enough. You are enough and you always have been. Life is beautiful, so make sure you're around to see it.

Lastly, I dedicate this book to my two nieces, Isla and Everly. Thank you for putting a smile on my face when I couldn't.

Olivia Daisy Phillips

SMOOTH LIKE WHISKEY

AUSTIN MACAULEY PUBLISHERS™

LONDON • CAMBRIDGE • NEW YORK • SHARJAH

A CIP catalogue record for this title is available from the British Library.

ISBN 9781398464483 (Paperback)
ISBN 9781398464490 (ePub e-book)

www.austinmacauley.com

First Published 2022
Austin Macauley Publishers Ltd®
1 Canada Square
Canary Wharf
London
E14 5AA

I want to thank my publishing team at Austin Macauley Publishers, for helping me make my dream a reality.

I want to thank my sister, Grace; brother, Ben; my brother-in-law, Oliver; Mum, Beverly; and Dad, Graham, for being my biggest supporters in anything I choose to do, and for listening to my ideas and encouraging me to write this book.
I have everything, because I have you.

Prologue
Bellamy

I cannot wait to get out of this place.

To be honest, I can't believe I was put here in the first place…no wait, actually I can but still…really? A psych ward.

The first thing I'm going to do is drink a cup of coffee, a proper cup of coffee, not the stupid excuse they call coffee here.

"Bellamy…Miss Edmondson," called the doctor. I could practically smell the coffee on his breath. Way to rub it in – I bet he didn't have to drink the swill they severed here. Lucky bastard.

"Sorry," I said, shaking myself back into the room. I couldn't help but stare at the obviously sleep deprived Dr Lockley's ugly tie and the stain on his sleeve. He looked how I felt.

"Are you okay, darling?" my mum asked, her eyes pleading with the emotion that only a mother can convey. The pain in her forced smile shattered my heart, no one should have to see their daughter like this.

"I'm fine, I just want to go home." I smiled back at Mum and gave her hand a squeeze, reassuring her I was okay because truly I was. I could feel it in my body that I was better.

I know and I understand that I will have days and fears that I need to overcome but I will do this. I can do this.

What I fear more than anything right now is having to sit and suffer through one of Dr Lockley's, *we can do this together,* speeches.

That would make anyone want to hit their head against a wall. Repeatedly, I assure you.

"Oh, of course, you do, we can't wait to have you home."

"As we discussed, we are going to discharge you on the medication we have been using here." He paused showing me the packets. I was handed two pills and he watched me swallow them.

Like a child.

"We are going to keep you on them for the foreseeable future. Then reassess the clinic in a few months. We recommend initially that these are to be controlled by Mum until you get into a stable routine."

As if I was tempted to take another OD and if I was, it wouldn't be with those tablets. But carry on talking to me like that. Because I'm obviously a 24-year-old child who cannot do anything for herself.

"Okay, Bellamy?" Dr Lockley asked in the most patronising voice. Oh, how I will miss that voice. NOT.

"Yes!" I saluted him, mocking him as my final farewell.

I was ready to get out of this stuffy, small office.

He seriously needed to get an air freshener maybe that should be his parting gift. Or deodorant and a mint.

Walking back to my room, I couldn't help thinking I might miss this place. There was no need to actually get dressed every day, I got to eat when I wanted, although I must say I won't miss their lasagne, I don't even think you could class it as lasagne just a bowl full of slop.

At least the ice cream was nice, which made up for the horrible food.

I didn't have my mum nagging me about my room or what I'm eating.

I might miss these four very boring yellow walls. The one very small window that never opened. Oh, to take a shower without a nurse peering over the awkwardly cut hole in the door to keep an eye on you. I could wash my bits in private, thank you.

What did they think I was hiding up there? I was 24 for fuck's sake.

24…blimey, how did I get here? Well, I know how I got here and I can't wait to get out.

"Bell, are you leaving?" I heard a very delicate and cautious voice coming from the door. It was Mary, she has been here on and off nearly all her life.

She was 36 and one of the kindest people I've ever met.

"I am." I smiled, turning to face her. The feeling was bittersweet having to say goodbye to my closest friend here.

"Promise me you'll try and get better?" I asked looking into her green eyes, I could see the pain behind them and knew what I was asking and how much it meant.

"I want to be able to spend some time with you out of this place." I could see tears forming in her eyes, crushing my heart.

"No, tears please, this is meant to be a happy day," I said, giving her a hug.

Hoping to transfer some of my slightly positive healing energy to her. My arms wrapped around her, all I could feel was bone.

I pray and hope she can get better. It was strange watching someone get better, you get to see them change into a new person, a different person, a better person, the person they were meant to be before they got ill and then sometimes for example in Mary's case you only got a glimpse of that person and then the illness would take over again.

"I will try, Bell, I promise." I knew it was a promise she could not keep. "And please come and visit, I don't think I can bear this place without you."

"Of course." I smiled.

"Besides you, I've only got my nan who visits and she's nearly deaf and blind." I couldn't help but laugh. Mary's nan was so lovely but having a conversation with her was extremely painful. Everyone knew the dementia was setting in but it did make the conversations slightly more entertaining.

The one person I didn't want to say goodbye too was Hallie, the therapy assistant. She was the kindest person I had ever met. For one she didn't talk to you like she was analysing all your past trauma. She spoke to you like a normal person, like she understood how broken I felt. I knocked on the door to her office and waited for her welcome me in.

"YEAH!" she shouted... Professional as ever.

"It's only me," I walked in, she immediately pulled her glasses off her face and I watched as her soft smile turned into a grin. She slammed her laptop shut and walked towards me swallowing me up in her arms.

"I mean this is the nicest way…" I heard her voice in my ear. "I never wanna see you here again," she finished, pulling away from me.

"Now, go live that life of yours and make it fucking amazing." Her grip was firm on my shoulders, her smile was infectious and it has helped me get through the last 6 weeks. After saying my final farewells, I was out of there. I cannot put into words the freedom I felt walking out those doors and feeling the cool air on my skin. I hope it will be the last time I ever have to exit those doors.

No, actually, I'm sure it will be the last time.

"I'm so happy to be free." I breathed in deep for what felt like the first time and gave my mum a huge hug.

"I've missed you," she said, rubbing my back. I could feel the emotion in my mum's movement, which was threatening to bring tears to my eyes. Inhaling her perfume and the smell of home washing detergent warmed my heart.

"I've missed you too, I promise I won't put you through all that again."

"Darling, it's okay," she reassured me.

"I love you, Mum."

"I love you too." I hope these words will be enough to carry me through this next recovery stage.

Chapter One
Two Years Later – Bellamy

I never thought at 26 I would be dancing to Shania Twain in my PJs whilst sipping my bottle of corona in my new flat after a long day of painting but, here we are and I wouldn't have it any other way. As the song came to an end, my heart was racing, threatening to beat out of my chest. I stopped to catch my breath and assessed my progress. Startled by a not so gentle nudge to the leg from Rover, my two-year-old golden retriever.

Life has changed a lot for me in the last two years and it's scary to sit back and think about it all, but regardless of the battle and many steps back, I'm grateful to be here.

A vibration from my phone on the makeshift ladder drew my attention to a Tinder message from Jonathan.

Please don't be weirdo, please don't be a weirdo. I pray to myself whilst loading the message.

Hello Bellamy, I must say I'd love to see your arse without those leggings.

Suppressing a groan, this was not the first message I've received like this. Doubting it would be the last from a horny creep. I scrolled up to the top and instantly pressed the unmatched button. This was the last straw and I deleted the app, admitting defeat.

Will I die an old overweight lady with five dogs? Yes.

Will I be happy about it? Yes.

Then again, it wouldn't hurt to have someone. Someone you can call your soul mate to share your life with, or even cry with.

To simply be loved and marry your best friend.

However, saying all this, I'm not sure what love is.

I don't think anyone has a clue what love is or even how to describe it.

Maybe that's the secret; it's not about our intellect, it's about something far deeper, far more hidden away than that. It's about just feeling it intuitively. Knowing that this is the person I want to spend my life with. I don't want to experience anything in my life now without this person. Maybe explaining love isn't the point, it's feeling it.

Maybe to fall in love or feel love isn't about someone. It's about appreciating all the little things.

The stars on a clear night. The smell of freshly mowed grass. The warmth of the sun on a summer evening or even as simple as the first sip of your morning coffee.

I crawled into bed, curling up with Rover and letting the exhaustion put me to sleep.

***

"Oh, crap." I didn't realise I had overslept and it's my niece's fourth birthday party in 20 minutes.

Cursing both my phone and my stupid brain for not turning the socket on!

What an idiot.

I kicked my legs out of the tangle that was my duvet and I rushed over to my bathroom.

Narrowly avoiding tripping over a snoring Rover who would be awake in seconds demanding food.

I jumped in the shower, brushed my teeth, and tried to comb through the mess of my pre-curled hair. Hastily applying some makeup so my mum doesn't comment on the heavy bags under my eyes and pale skin.

I chuck on a pair of jeans, a patterned light blue blouse and my white vans. I quickly fed Rover and headed out the door.

I've mastered the art of getting ready in a short amount of time ever since I was at school. I would wake up 15 minutes before I had to leave. Mainly because my sister or brothers would be hogging the bathroom so I had to adjust to their schedule.

I jumped into my truck, turned the engine on, forgetting how loud I had my country music on last night until it came blaring through the sound system. Who needed caffeine if that was my morning wake up? With that in mind, I mentally plotted my route to the nearest drive-through Starbucks.

Then, all of a sudden, a thought hit me. Not only did I forget the present, but I also forgot the dog. Turning my engine off, I ran back to unlock the door. Rover was already there waiting for me, sulking. I looked down at his food bowl to see it was already suspiciously empty. Pig. "Don't look at me like that. You're lucky you're coming," I groaned as he ran over to the truck.

I got Rover two years ago. I came home from the hospital and found a mischievous golden retriever puppy on my bed. He was sitting there cute as a button, chewing the throw that was neatly thrown onto my bed. He was definitely my dog from the start. Mum and Dad thought getting a dog would be the best thing for me and they were right. All parents have that annoying habit of being right. Especially when you don't want them to be.

I parked directly opposite my sister's house, noting how many other cars surrounded the property and how late I was. I hastily exited the car with Rover at my heels resisting the urge to run ahead to the awaited treats.

"Auntie!" I heard a sweet delicate voice call me as I rang the doorbell. It never quite feels real when you become an auntie.

I remember the day Libby was born, getting a face time at 2:34 am to meet a sleeping bald baby and she was beautiful. She was so small, weighing 6lb 10oz. When I first met her, she was buried in a pink blanket with her eyes closed.

"Happy birthday! How is the birthday girl?" I asked crouching down to her level seeing the sparkle and joy in her young eyes.

Libby had beautiful long platinum blonde hair that fell past her shoulders, she had big blue eyes that she got from my brother-in-law and thankfully for her, she didn't inherit the Edmondson's nose. Unlike some, aka me.

"Is that my present?" she asked, her whole body vibrating with excitement as her body bobbed with anticipation.

"Yes, it is," I said smiling and she ran inside to tell everyone just how big her present was.

Walking through the door, Rover barged past me to get to my family. He was so impatient. They always had food waiting for him, at times I think he likes them more than me for purely that reason.

"Hey everyone!" I shouted through the hallway.

This was followed by my sister Alice waddling around the corner with her pregnant tummy protruding.

People say you glow during pregnancy...Maybe women do...but not my sister.

She was the queen of grumpy. I guess anyone would be if they had a baby playing football with their bladder and internal organs but still you wanted a baby therefore, toughen up buttercup. However, saying all this I couldn't wait to be a mum one day.

"Hey, Bell, how are you?" she said with a smile. My sister had the most beautiful brown hair that fell off her shoulders in a natural wave. Alice is a natural beauty and I have always been jealous of her, she has such a huge, loving, kind heart. Apart from Iris, was my best friend.

"Still no man on your arm I see," my mum commented with disappointment.

I have a question: why did my value as a daughter have to come from having a man on my arm? Not my multiple qualifications? Or the fact that I regularly helped save lives?

"Or lady," Thomas corrected her.

"Thomas!" Alice yelled as he ducked back into the kitchen to avoid the nearest projectile I was likely to throw at him. He was lucky my mum stood in the way of him and the orange that was sitting alone in the fruit bowl.

"Hello, Darling," my mum then spoke in her sweet voice kissing me on the cheek.

"Hi, Mum," I replied with a slightly tight-lipped smile.

"Here, let me take that," Thomas said, grinning, knowing Libby would love the present or the box it came in. Honestly, I don't know what it was that I bought her but it was on Libby's wish list. It was very pink, very big and very expensive.

Thomas and Alice have only been married for two years, but have been together for seven.

Thomas was nine years older than Alice. He always said to me that he would rather turn 50 alone and single than be with someone he knew deep down wasn't his true love.

It just so happens that Alice walked into his life at the age of 35 and he knew she was the one.

Their love and bond was what made me believe in true love and to know it's okay to wait until you find the right one.

They were each other's soul mates and I couldn't wait to have something like that one day. Let's just hope I don't have to wait till I'm 35.

"So, how is everyone?" I asked, hopefully saving myself from further examination…

"Grubs up!" Dad yelled from the Kitchen, thankfully saving me from the inquisition. He had great timing. My hero.

As it was Libby's special day, therefore, she got to choose what we all had for lunch – this year she decided on Grandad's famous roast dinner. Despite it being 25 degrees in mid-June, it probably wasn't the best idea but a roast was always welcome, especially my dad's.

Besides, no one could say no to her pretty blue eyes, apart from her mum.

My dad has this magical gift of being able to make anyone laugh.

He stood at 6 foot 3, with ginger hair, and he was my favourite person.

My family was large and I loved every single one of them. I was extremely lucky to have them, they aren't just my family but they are friends.

Firstly, was William, who was my eldest brother, who was married to Sarah. They had twin boys three years ago, Austin and Liam. Next was heavily pregnant Alice as I pointed out previously, who was married to Thomas with little Libby.

There was my other brother, Alexander, who was currently in the army and managed to avoid the majority of mum's scrutiny, but ended up with our nans for 'volunteering' to go 'headfirst into a bloody war'.

Lastly, there was me, Bellamy Edmondson the youngest, possibly the loudest, clumsiest of the bunch.

When we were younger, we argued all the time but if someone was picking on any of us, you bet your arse you wouldn't see the light of day again.

Especially with Alexander and his legal access to weapons.

Thankfully now, we are all the best of friends and I wouldn't have it any other way.

"You know you can breathe in-between bites!" Alice snapped, she was suffering from awful nausea which meant she was stuck on bland food and small portions. Not that it was my problem but we all had to suffer for it.

"Plus, it's not very lady-like to eat like that." Mum chimed in too, looking at me with disapproval written all over her face. Did that look come naturally with having children? Alice had mastered it already. So, with that comment, I made direct eye contact with her and opened my mouth and stuffed a

20

whole potato in. Libby giggled at my actions, which were cut off by a stern glare from Alice in case she got any ideas.

I was obviously my nieces' favourite. If that wasn't clear before.

"Blimey," Mum huffed, irritated whilst Dad was winking at her across the table.

"And she wonders why she's single," William laughed, earning him a clip across the ear.

"Well, you're definitely your father's daughter," Sarah laughed.

"Why thank you!" I beamed. What a compliment.

"Are you excited about your holiday? Aren't you going away with Iris?" Sarah asked, quickly changing the subject. Twice in less than an hour, they brought up my relationship status – sadly still off their personal best. Which were five times.

"Yeah! Three weeks and counting! I'm so excited" – I paused for a second forgetting what I also will be missing – "It will be weird being in Portugal without you guys though." It was an annual tradition for us to all visit Portugal together.

The same place.

The same villa. Every year.

It was our second home. It started with my nan going when she was little and then taking Mum. The rest was history. We are lucky enough to know most of the locals and they have all become our Portuguese family.

"You might meet someone," Thomas said, suggestively wiggling his eyebrows.

I snorted, narrowly avoiding spraying my water everywhere.

"I highly doubt that."

"I highly doubt it too," Alice said, speaking over everyone.

I glared at her, waiting for her to explain.

"What? Don't look at me like that, we all know what she's like. I'm not being funny, Bell and don't take this personally but you don't exactly. You know..." she said, shoving another bit of crispy potato in her mouth.

That's the thing about the sentence, *don't take this personally*, which means yes, I will take this personally and you are probably going to insult me.

Here we go.

"Know what?" I said challenging her.

"You've worked so hard to lose weight and you always cover up your body. Whenever a guy shows any interest in you, you instantly beat them away like flies because you cannot believe in yourself enough to understand that men can and are interested in you." I let Alice finish her rant.

I dwelled on it for a second, thinking maybe she's right but I can't help it. It's very hard to change that way of thinking.

I see it at the gym all the time, a guy smiles at me and then when a fit, prettier one comes along you get forgotten. I don't take it personally, it's just the way life is.

I see it every day, so I just got used to the facts of life and how men are and how they think. Plus, I don't think most of them like the fact I'm stronger than them.

"I am more than happy with how I am and how I dress. Thank you very much. I am not confident and I refuse to parade my body around in a bikini when I don't have and will never have that sort of body" – I took a breath then continued

– "I do not batter men away, I just simply haven't met the right person—"

"That's because you don't give them a chance." Alice cut me off.

I looked over at my dad for help or anyone really that will sweep in and rescue me.

No one's gonna help me? No one?

"Oh, for God's sake!" I huffed.

"Don't get upset, Bell, you just don't have the best track record with men, I just worry about you and your future," Mum said.

"I'm more than aware, thank you, but I'm fine, okay? I'm fine," I said, raising my voice.

"She's fine," William said, mocking me with his hands flaring.

That deserved a kick under the table.

"Ouch," he moaned, feeling my foot dig into his calf.

"Who needs a man when you can have potatoes?" Libby said.

"Exactly, see," I said, high-fiving my niece.

"Girls are stupid," Austin, the youngest twin, said making Liam laugh, causing broccoli to come flying out his mouth.

Gross.

"Liam." Sarah sculled wiping away the mess.

"No, we are not!" Libby shouted.

"Are too!" Austin shouted back.

"Are not!" Libby defending herself.

"Yes!" Austin replied.

"Enough!" Sarah shouted at both of them.

"The guests will be arriving soon and if you do not start behaving, you won't be having any of Libby's Birthday cake," Sarah said to the twins.

Leaving Libby to sit there smiling.

"That includes you too Libby, birthday girl or not," Alice scolded.

"I understand about 20% of what goes on around here," Dad mumbled, taking a sip out of his beer bottle.

The guests soon started to arrive, the house quickly turned into a circus.

There were screaming kids everywhere. It was quite funny watching Sarah and Alice try to tame them all.

"Thought you might want one of these." My knight in shining armour. My dad with two beers in his hands.

"Oh yes please, thank you," I said, taking a sip.

"Don't take it to heart, Bell, you know what they are like, they just want the best for you, as we all do."

"I know, Dad and trust me I would love to meet someone but I just haven't yet and I'm not worried or rushing into anything."

"I know that and I understand that trust me I do, you can take all the time in the world. Your mum and I are still paying off Alice's wedding dress."

"I knew you paid for that bloody dress," I muttered while taking another sip of my beer.

"Don't tell your mother I told you."

I raised my beer and he acknowledged that his secret was safe with me. He kissed me on the forehead and then joined the kids on the bouncy castle. This will be interesting.

Chapter Two
Bellamy

The party was finally over and I was ready to leave. Actually, I was ready two hours ago.

I had been dragged into playing tag with the children and then Libby wanted me to learn her new birthday dance, I was done. My aunt's duties were over for the day. My back ached, my hair was currently flying all over the place, and my mascara was smeared down my eyes from laughing too much. I looked like a mess, I kinda felt like a mess too.

Pulling up to my flat I looked over to Rover. I bent over and gave him a kiss on the forehead, which led him to give me a slobbery kiss in return on the cheek.

Once we were in my flat, I slipped my vans off and took my bra off.

I couldn't help but feel sorry for men that they don't get to enjoy this sort of pleasure when you can just let the boobs hang free.

I got into my cow print pyjamas. I poured myself a warm cup of tea and looked at the mess in my flat.

I had a lot of boxes to unpack.

When you walked through the front door, the lounge and kitchen were open plan. I had a cream L-shaped sofa that faced a 50-inch TV and a glass coffee table separating the two with a huge cream boho rug underneath. My sofa was lined with eight scatter pillows and a throw that was spread out.

The kitchen was open and facing into the lounge. There were all-white cupboards with gold long handles with white marble counters. I had plants lining up the first shelf, two succulents, aloe vera and a cactus.

I named them all, obviously.

Aragon, Sheldon, Thor and Spike.

The bathroom was very basic. White tiles covered the walls and floors. I had a bath, toilet and sink. Nothing exciting, but it was all mine.

Luckily, for me, it was on the ground floor so I was able to have a small garden. There was a window by the sink that looked out to the garden. I had solar fairy lights everywhere, reaching from one end of the garden to the other. It was small but perfect for Rover to go out, have a sniff and do his business.

The bedroom was big, simple white walls, dark brown wooden flooring that traced the whole flat.

A king-sized white ottoman bed sat in the middle of the room with a sign above saying:

Country roads take me home.

With oversized pillows lining the headboard and a fluffy throw two sizes too big. Then there stood a large eight-foot mirror. I bought it at a vintage store and spray painted it white. It was the most expensive thing I owned. Minus the big fluffy dog barking at the back door to come in.

After Rover and I settled in bed, I turned on a documentary and we both fell asleep.

***

Stretching to press on the snooze button a huge yawn escaped my mouth. I looked over at my uniform neatly pressed on my radiator. I still couldn't believe I was able to fit into a size 12.

This time two years ago I was a size 20 eating my feelings every night. After losing my job and being dumped by who I thought was the love of my life.

The world around me seemed like it was falling apart.

Slowly, everything turned black, even my heart.

I spiralled into a bad depression and was constantly fighting with suicidal thoughts. It got to the point where I wasn't allowed on my own, my mum confiscated my razors and my tablets, she only gave me them when needed. I ended up in the hospital one night after I tried to take my own life, that's when I was sent to a psych ward for 6 weeks. It was a hard time, not just for me but for my whole family and friends. I will never forget the look on their faces when I woke up in the hospital. I begged for them to leave me alone, let me die because I wanted to be at peace. Fighting with your brain every day was exhausting, but it got better, it took time but it got better.

Once I got my life back together, I decided to get back into the gym and it changed my life. I went from a size 20 with no self-esteem to lifting weights I didn't know my body was capable of lifting. I became my own kind of beautiful.

The only thing left from my previous life was the stretch marks travelling from my pelvis to the middle of my stomach, by my waist across my bum and around the tops of my arms.

Most of them have faded now, but catch them in the right light and you'll see every imperfection tracing my skin. Maybe they are the reason why I haven't been with anyone since my ex. I was embarrassed about my stretch marks and sagging skin. I just couldn't see myself allowing another person to love me when I still hated so many different things about the way I look.

Hey girl I'm leaving mine in five, see you soon x, my phone buzzed from the incoming text from my best friend Iris, distracting me from my thoughts. I had a very quick shower and shoved my long blonde hair in a messy bun. I nearly forgot to feed the dog until a loud bark erupted from his mouth.

I heard Iris pulling up to my flat. The loud music giving her away.

I grabbed my bag, coat, gave Rover a kiss, telling him the dog walker will be here in a couple of hours and I headed out the door.

"Girl, you look like shit, are you okay?" another thing I loved about Iris was her brutal honesty.

"I hardly slept last night," I replied laughing, rubbing my sleepy eyes.

"You're not getting bad again, are you? You haven't been sleeping well the past couple of weeks and I worry about you."

"No, I'm okay you know how things get. That reminds me I need to thank Maeve for letting me have a job at the pub. This is really gonna help me out," I said.

"Don't mention it, you're my best friend plus it will be nice to have someone on my shift I actually like. Maeve is also getting someone new in for lockdown every night. I think it's her nephew or someone but apparently, he is fucking gorgeous but he won't be here till the New Year." I smiled back, rolling my eyes.

I bloody loved this girl and her no shame slaggy ness.

Reaching up to the hospital we exit the car ready for another crazy day of saving lives.

I started my job as a Health Care Assistant only three months ago.

I'm currently working in the dementia ward and it was horrific.

It was a daily battle of watching someone disappear, not so much physically at first but mentally. Watching their loved ones come in and their hope disappear from their eyes as their mother forgot who they were today.

"Morning girls!" the barista Val shouted over the counter.

Her husband has been staying in the dementia ward for the past three weeks. They have been married for 35 years, she told me one day whilst I was taking his blood pressure. "Look after my man now, Miss," she said winking at me with her sweet smile full of hope.

"Of course, I will." I smiled taking one last look at her wrinkled face and short grey hair. She looked tired today, but she still managed to put on some makeup and pink lipstick. If I looked like her at her age, I'd be happy.

"He is getting worse," I whispered to Iris, turning the corner to where we usually part.

"They always do, but I know you are the best person for the job to keep them as comfortable as possible till the very end. Have a good day and I'll see you at lunch," she said, kissing my cheek and turning into the ER.

She was amazing and passionate about her job. It was truly inspiring. She was one of the main reasons I went into healthcare, I wanted to help, I wanted to make a difference like she did. My next big step is the paramedic interview I was hoping to get that I applied for a couple of months back.

After the first crazy four hours of my day, I knew I needed a break, I walked down to the cafe, took out my homemade pesto pasta and dug in.

"That's not very lady-like," Iris chuckled walking up to the table.

"Why does everyone keep saying this?" I struggled to say with a mouth full of pasta.

"Only three weeks and then we are away to Portugal, I cannot wait!" Iris beamed.

"Me either I cannot believe this will be our first holiday," I said, shaking my head and brushing the hair out of my face.

Iris and I have been best friends for over 20 years.

We are two completely different people in every way, shape and form but someone we just worked. She was the yin to my yang.

"I need to get some Vitamin D," Iris said, winking at me.

"God, I'm glad we've got our own rooms," I snorted, eating more of my pasta.

"Maybe you could get a little bit of action for once, you know, blow away the cobwebs," she whispered, nodding to my groan.

"Not gonna happen, Romeo," I said smiling.

"Yeah, we'll see," she said, raising her eyebrows.

"Hey ladies," said Michael, a trainee surgeon.

30

Chapter Three
Three Weeks Later – Bellamy

The pilot released the seatbelt signs and immediately everyone rushed to their feet, grabbing their phones and bags. Talking with anticipation of getting out of the plane and starting their holiday. Luckily for us, we were at the top of the plane so we chilled out until the doors opened, much to the annoyance of everyone else.

Iris reluctantly closed her romance book and lowered her glasses, taking slow sips of her tea with her pinkie hanging out for dramatic effect.

"Okay girl, let's do this," Iris said, finally pulling her bag from the overhead locker as the door opened. They slowly opened the doors to the plane. We were hit by a wall of heat and it was welcomed with open arms.

I needed more caffeine – been awake since 3 am and it wasn't even a bloody night shift. We walked through the terminal, went through passport control and now we are just waiting for our luggage, which sometimes seems to be the longest part.

I looked around the airport waiting for the TV to show that our luggage was now being sorted. Minding my own business nice and peacefully until I noticed a familiar face.

Then it hit me.

It was Jack, my ex.

I had to double look at first but yes that was definitely him.

"Shit," I muttered ducking behind Iris.

"What the…" Iris said looking back at me.

"What the hell are you doing?" she said looking at me I just pointed my finger. Iris followed my arm and then her eyes found Jack.

"Oh, shit!" she said, her body language said she was ready to pounce on him even if it got her arrested and banned from this country. She would still say it was worth it to knock the smug smile off his face and correct his unbroken nose.

"That's what I said!" I pointed out, still trying to hide behind her.

The last time I saw him he left me standing outside my parents' house crying.

"Bellamy, what are you doing here?" Jack smiled, closing the distance between us.

I popped out behind Iris.

"Hello, Jack," I muttered.

"Hey B. Iris, you look beautiful as always," Jack's Best friend Marcus said.

Iris was so beautiful, with her long dark brown hair that reached her bum. Beautiful big green eyes, long thick eyelashes, a tiny waist and the most wonderful personality.

"Where are all the other guys?" Iris asked looking behind them.

"Oh, they are all coming tomorrow, big boys' holiday," Marcus answered.

My eyes wandered over to Jack to see he was already looking at me and I felt sick, not with sadness or nervousness but with anger.

Pure anger.

"Some people may call this fate," Jack said with a smirk.

"Or a living nightmare," I said, grabbing Iris's hand and walking her over to the other side of the carousel.

"What is he doing here?" Iris asked.

"I don't bloody know," I hissed looking over at him again.

"Oh, I see our luggage." Iris pointed.

"Fantastic," I said, yanking the bags from the carousel and practically running out of the airport.

***

"Thank you so much." I smiled at the taxi driver passing him a tip of 20 euros. I didn't realise how hot it was until we exited the air-conditioned taxi.

"It's so lovely here, I'm ready to get a tan and get drunk." Iris laughed over my shoulder.

"Couldn't agree more," I admitted.

Our apartment was opposite the reception, which had a tennis court, gym and another big pool to the left. There were four pools around the resort and our apartment was right by the biggest pool that had a bar to the right and a restaurant.

Opening up the doors. The apartment had white walls, white floor tiles, two yellow sofas that pointed to a small TV and fireplace. A small open-plan kitchen was hidden in the corner of the apartment.

I've been here before, not this exact apartment but this resort.

It was my 18th birthday when Mum and Dad surprised me with a weekend away to Portugal with the rest of the family.

"Oh my God, Bell, we are so close to the pool, look at the view." Iris looked out from the porch doors, jumping with excitement.

"It's lovely, isn't it? Which room do you want?" I asked.

"Erm, that one." She pointed to the room on the left.

"Cool, meet out here in an hour and then we'll go and look around. It looks like past the pool there's a walkway to the beach," I said meeting Iris at the porch doors.

"Sounds perfect," Iris said, walking into her room as I retreated to mine.

The cleaners left all the windows slightly open and the breeze felt too good to be true. I looked through the window and this view drew the biggest smile on my face.

My room was facing the ocean, trees and bushes stood in the way from the perfect view but it was good enough for me. I couldn't see the pool from here but I could hear children laughing and the distant chatter of adults.

I dragged off my joggers, crop top and trainers.

I was ready to get into a pair of shorts and sandals.

I opened up my suitcase. And pulled out all my tops, shorts, dresses, swimwear, underwear and organised it all in their separate piles. If there's one thing I like being, it was organised.

I wore my Levi shorts that I bought a size too big just to make myself feel better.

I slipped in a flowy red Bardot and I swept my hair into a messy bun. I looked at myself in the mirror and I couldn't help but look at my legs. I've always had bigger legs and it was always such a big insecurity for me but I took my sister's advice and bought shorts, four dresses and whatever she made me buy on our shopping trip. We were only an hour in when I just gave her my card and waited in the car.

Once we were both ready, we left the apartment and I walked Iris to a bar called Stove, which had the best burgers. We sat there in the sun; it was lovely looking up at the bright blue sky with no clouds in sight. The sand was golden and there was no end to the horizon.

There was no other background music but the waves and distant chatter. It was so peaceful, just what I needed.

Loud laughter interrupted my thoughts and brought me back to reality. A group of four boys who clearly had been drinking since the early hours as one could not walk in a straight line.

"Good afternoon, could we book a table for four, please?" the brown-headed, unshaven, over six-foot man spoke in a deep Scottish voice.

I was unable to peel my eyes off him.

He had a gentle face with a sharp jawline, I couldn't quite describe it but he was striking and very easy on the eyes. His blue eyes looked around and landed straight on me.

Shit, I immediately turned away.

"They are fit," Iris whispered over the table.

"Yup," I muttered looking back at Iris, sipping my wine.

We soon finished our meals and were two bottles down so we decided to leave and head back to the apartment. I couldn't help myself but take another glance over at the brown-haired man, who was too busy laughing with his friends. I was so fascinated, it was like magic. At that point, a tornado of butterflies was set alight in my tummy.

"I haven't laughed like that in such a long time," I said, taking in a deep breath as I looked in my bag for the keys.

"It's nice seeing a smile on your face," Iris said hugging me goodnight.

We decided to have an early night as the travelling and alcohol took it out on us.

Departing into our bedrooms I turned on the fan, took my makeup off and let the alcohol send me to sleep.

***

The morning soon came and I was up at six reading my book in bed. Dragging myself from the comfy bedding, I poured my morning coffee and a cuppa tea for Iris trying to prevent her loud voice from moaning, *I cannot do anything until I have a cuppa.*

After I finished my coffee, I laid all my swimwear out. I had no clue what to wear.

If I show too much boob, will I look slutty? Or if I show less boob will I look boring?

Sometimes I hated being a woman.

After spending the next 20 minutes wondering what won't make me look slaggy, fat, hideous, or frigid, I chose my lucky black strapless two pieces. I never wore bikinis only because of my belly and stretch marks. The black thonged bottoms covered my belly button so I knew no stretch marks and flab would be on show.

"You fitty!" Iris shouted from my doorframe.

I laughed giving myself a final check in the mirror as I put my hair in a high messy bun.

I could stand here all day looking at myself, picking out things I didn't like about what I saw. I couldn't help but notice Iris's amazing figure. She wore a hot pink bikini and looked like a Victoria secret model.

"I don't think you realise how much weight you've lost. You look amazing, I mean it!" she said, grabbing my shoulders. I could tell she sensed my anxiety. She knew me better than I knew myself most of the time.

Our apartment led out towards the pool so it wasn't a far walk. Iris placed herself softly onto the sunbed letting her beautiful body catch the sun's late morning rays. On the other hand, I still had my kimono on and it was going to stay on. I crossed my legs, put on my headphones and listened to my audiobook, *talking with serial killers*.

A couple hours later, I heard loud noises coming from the bar and there to my surprise was the guy from the cafe and all of his friends.

"Now we are talking," Iris said, looking over her sunglasses.

As in slow motion, the four men from the cafe yesterday all walked towards the pool and towards the four beds with towels already laid out. Which placed them right opposite us.

Within a second, he was slipping his top off. My eyes wandered very slowly up from his waist all the up past his shoulders towards his face. He wasn't hugely built but you could tell he worked out. He was not the pretty boy kind of handsome but the rough kind that you just knew he'd break your heart.

Oh God. I think I need to take a long, very cold shower.

I put my headphones back on and relaxed onto the bed, trying to ignore the ache in my groin. "Take it off!" Iris said, smacking my arm.

"What?" I said yanking off my headphones.

"Take off that stupid kimono and show off that beautiful body you worked so hard to get, don't think I didn't notice you eye fucking the Scottish. Now, Bellamy Edmondson, if you will do one thing for me, take it off."

"Are you crazy?" I replied, feeling the heat rush to my cheeks.

"You're being ridiculous, I'm going to get us a cocktail," she said lifting her shades back on her eyes.

I watched as Iris took the long way around catching the eye of the boys sitting opposite us. Except for the brown-haired, mysterious stranger who was looking at me. Heat rushed to my face and I laid back down on the sunbed waiting for Iris to return.

"Holy shit." Iris came rushing back with two strawberry daiquiris in her hand. "You never guess who's here?" she whispered.

"Lucifer?" I replied.

"No, Jack and Marcus."

"Just what I need." I grabbed the cocktail from her hand sipping through the straw, looking over to see where Jack was. There they are, on the sunbeds at the far right. Now if they could move farther away I'd really appreciate it, maybe closer to the sea? Or possibly just piss off back to England.

Jack and Marcus are two very good-looking men, it's just a shame their personalities sucked.

Two hours later, we were five cocktails down.

"You know what fuck it," I said standing up from the bed, feeling slightly uneasy on my feet.

"Excuse me?" Iris said, looking over at me.

"I'm not gonna do this to myself." I took a deep breath and slowly lifted the kimono from my legs, all the way over my head letting anyone and everyone see my not so perfect bikini body.

It was definitely the drink talking and taking action but I didn't care. I threw it on the bed, letting my hair down and looked over at Iris whose mouth was gaping open. "So apparently pigs do fly!" she said, clapping her hands.

I looked around nervously and I saw Jack staring at me. He made me so mad with just one look and I wanted to walk over and punch him in his stupid face. I pulled my purse out of my bag and I was ready for another cocktail or four. I glanced down at my kimono and decided not to put it back on. I slipped my flip-flops on and I walked over to the bar and ordered two sexes on the beach and two mojitos.

"You look amazing." I noticed the voice immediately.

Here we go.

"Thanks," I said to Jack not looking at him.

"I mean it, you look great," he said, lightly touching my arm.

I looked up at him and yanked it back.

"And I mean it when I say if you ever touch me again I will punch you in the throat." I grabbed the tray from the bar and marched over to Iris.

"Jump in the pool with me," I said smiling from ear to ear placing the cocktails on the table.

"I thought you'd never ask," Iris said, lifting herself up from the bed.

We leapt into the pool. I allowed the water to develop my body. I reluctantly reached for the surface. It felt as if the cool water was baptising me, washing away all the anxiety and doubt I was feeling.

Chapter Four
Later That Day – Bellamy

I slipped on the one-shoulder skin-tight black dress Alice made me buy and to my surprise; I didn't hate it. I put my hair in a low ponytail and applied a light layer of makeup to my face and then traced my lips with bright, hot, red lipstick. I was ready for our first night out.

"Oh, Mamma Mia!" I heard Iris shouting from the door.

"What do ya think?" I asked spinning, showing her the whole look.

"You look beautiful."

"As do you," I said, looking at her in a deep red strappy dress.

"Oh, what this old thing," she said in a southern accent flipping her long hair off her shoulder.

We both walked past the pool towards the bar. We decided to stay at the resort tonight. The sun was setting leaving the sky a beautiful colour of pink and orange. I immediately noticed the four men and my eyes immediately darted to him.

"Earth to Bellamy." I heard from afar, looking over at Iris who was already at the bar ordering us a drink.

"Sorry," I said walking over.

"Shall I get the table whilst you get the drinks?" I asked.

"Yeah, sure." She smiled.

I walked over to the man who was standing at the entrance to the tables with a clipboard.

He looked tired and extremely hot in his suit and bow tie.

"Hi, reservation for Bellamy please." I smiled.

"Ah yes, right this way." I looked at Iris and tried waving my hand to get her to notice me, but she was preoccupied with a blonde guy, a very tall handsome blonde guy, laughing away sipping out of her glass.

She was really good, I'm pretty sure she could chat up a tree.

Sitting down at the table set for two. I looked around at the beautiful scenery and heard the water crash against the rocks. A light breeze drove past my face and it felt refreshing on my slightly burnt shoulders.

"Hey, sorry about that, I was just chatting to that guy." Iris nodded over to the man and took the seat opposite me.

"His name is Scott," she said with excitement.

"Oh really?" I replied raising my eyebrows.

"Yeah, and he said he's gonna buy me a drink later." She winked.

As time went on, I was getting drunker. I was extremely full from the three courses we just demolished and I left Iris dancing with Scott by the pool. I give them another 10 minutes and they'll be kissing. I was getting fed up sitting here like a loser so I got up from the table and headed to the bar and ordered a whiskey.

Half an hour went past and Iris was still with Scott and I was more than happy over here with my drink and being left alone.

"Hey." I heard Jack's voice from behind me, I could smell his aftershave and it brought back so many memories.

And now I'm not alone anymore. Splendid.

"Hi Jack," I said without turning around.

I heard his mate Marcus order a drink and Jack slipped onto the barstool next to me.

"I'm sorry about earlier. It's good to see you. I hardly recognised you tonight," he said.

"That's the point, how may I help you?" I asked, finally turning towards him. Signalling the barman to top up my glass. For a second, I forgot how handsome he was. I remember those eyes waking me up most mornings with a gentle smile.

Snap out of it, Bellamy.

"Listen, I'm sorry, I didn't get in contact with you, once I knew you were in the hospital, I was so shocked I didn't know you were suffering so much." Before he could finish his sentence, I jumped in.

"How's Brooke?" I said with a blank expression on my face gulping down the liquid from my recently filled up glass.

She was everything I wasn't.

Had an amazing job up in London, a BMW, a petite little body, perfectly manicured fingers.

I could go on but let's not dwell on the past. I didn't have a grudge on her, not really. She just fell for the brown eyes and beautiful words just like I did.

"We aren't together anymore, we broke up last month."

"Now, isn't that a tragic story," I replied.

"It's been tough but every day gets better."

He had sadness in his eyes, which made me think he possibly did truly love her and maybe he was heartbroken like

I was a couple of years ago. But I didn't want to sit here and listen to this sob story.

"Don't worry about it, I understand whilst I was having a mental breakdown you were still trying to navigate your girlfriend's clitoris, cause hell you couldn't find mine, now if you don't mind, I'm enjoying a nice peaceful drink on my own." I snapped turning back to face the bar. They grabbed their drinks and swiftly retreated back to their table.

Thank God.

The bar was massive, which sat next to the outdoor restaurant that had fairy lights stringing from one beam to another. The upbeat music was blaring through the speakers and the glowing colourful lights were flashing in unison. Going from blue to green, pink, purple back to blue. It was mesmerising. I couldn't help but want to jump in the massive pool that was glowing in the moonlight.

"Girl, you are mean." I heard a voice coming from the right of me.

There he was the mysterious stranger.

I wanted to comb my fingers through his thick hair and feel his stubble against my cheek when we kissed. He was wearing an oversized black shirt that had the first three buttons undone and matching black shorts.

"Well, he had it coming to him." I shrugged my shoulders trying to play it cool as I took a big gulp of my whiskey, letting it burn my throat on the way down.

"That bad?" he asked.

"You have no idea," I laughed placing the glass on the bar.

"Are you here all on your own?"

"No, I came here with my best mate who is currently right over there," I said, pointing my finger to Iris kissing Scott.

"Ah yes, he kept on going on about the beautiful girl from the pool. He's a good guy, he just thinks with his dick."

"Don't most men do that?" I laughed.

"Yeah most of them I hate to admit, just remind me to never get on your bad side." He smiled and chuckled while drinking his beer.

"My name is Mark," he said, reaching out one hand.

Alas, he has a name.

"I'm Bellamy." I reached over with my left hand, leaning on one side of the stool, which wasn't a good idea because before I knew it the chair leg gave way and my face met the floor with a massive *thud*.

"Are you okay?" I heard Mark's voice in worry, bending down to come to my level.

Which was currently very close to the floor.

"Yep, all good," I muttered trying to pull myself back up, dusting off my dress.

Only me.

ONLY ME.

"Believe me, this happens to me more often than I care to admit," I said laughing at myself, trying to hide how embarrassed I was beginning to feel.

"Anyway," I said, grabbing my purse from the counter, I think it was best I left before I embarrass myself further.

"It's time I went back to the apartment," I said opening my purse. "Found it." I yanked some money out of my purse and handed it to the waiter.

"There you go." I smiled.

47

"And you" – I said pointing to Mark – "I will see you later." I took a deep breath.

Can I stand?

Yes.

Can I walk? Yes, okay, this is good can I walk straight?

Okay, not so much but we'll get there.

Mark:

I sat there and watched Bellamy try and walk away but I couldn't stand there and let her walk back to the apartment alone, especially in her current state.

"Okay nope," I muttered to myself, handing the bartender some money and running to her side.

"Careful," I said grabbing her arm and steadying her on her feet.

"Holy shit balls!" Bellamy jumped, her hand coming to her chest.

"Holy shit balls?" I questioned trying not to laugh.

"You scared me." She sighed.

"I'm sorry," I said, letting go of her arm making sure she was steady.

"I think I should walk you back to your door."

"No, it's good, it's literally up there," she said, pointing into the distance.

"You say that but you just fell off a stool and nearly went for a midnight swim," I said looking over to the pool that was to her right.

"Okay, okay but just this once," she said lifting one finger in the air.

"Yes, ma'am, I swear," I said hand on my heart.

I led her up the path and then she stopped.

"This is me." She pointed to the porch doors.

"You weren't kidding when you said it was literally up there," I chuckled.

"No, I was not." She went to put the key in the door and then stopped.

"Oh bollocks," she said kicking the door.

"What?" I asked.

"I forgot my friend." Her head then hit the door and her arm flew over to the lady who was with Scott.

"Okay, you stay here," I ordered then ran off to get her friend.

Once I delivered the friend to Bellamy, she unlocked the door and they both filed in. I began to walk back to the bar until I heard a whisper from the door.

"Mark, wait!" Bellamy's head popped out behind the curtain.

"Yes?" I said turning around, my eyes meeting hers.

"Thank you," she said before going back behind the curtain and locking the door.

A smile crossed my face, it might be the drink, the stars in the sky or it could be the beautiful woman I just walked back to her apartment.

Bellamy.

Beautiful, Bellamy.

I have been so lucky to call Portugal my home for the past five weeks.

I don't know why I thought Portugal would be the best place to escape too but it called to me. I've been to many places, Greece, Italy, and America. I even went to Russia four years ago just to experience it. Portugal seemed the next beautiful place to be.

I've been living in this complex since I got here.

It wasn't a true holiday until the boys arrived.

We've been a foursome ever since we were in school. We went to the same college. Even when Bill and Scott went to university, we still played FIFA on Friday nights.

Chapter Five
Bellamy

Waking up to the early morning sunrise peeking through the shutters I couldn't help but smile…and then came the pounding from last night's drinks. That smile quickly turned into a frown.

"Only 6:30," I said, wiping the sleep from my eyes, looking at my watch.

I stumbled into the kitchen and poured myself a large coffee, allowing the smell to reach my nose and it was marvellous.

I walked over and unlocked the porch doors. Letting the morning breeze slowly wake me up. I plopped myself on the wall separating our apartment from the pathway leading to the pool, which most people used during the day but this early in the morning it was quiet and peaceful. I leaned back against the wall and laid my feet up on the side, hugging the warm mug close to my chest. It doesn't matter how hot it gets here during the day, the mornings were always a little bit chilly. Mid-sip I looked up and in the distance, I saw a topless man running towards me…

As he got closer and closer, I noticed it was Mark. I went to sip my coffee not realising my mouth was not engaging with my brain, and a mouthful of hot liquid spilt down my chest.

"Shit!" I yelped, trying to wipe off the boiling coffee from my skin. Tossing my head up realising how loud I was, Mark stopped running and looked around.

In an urgent need to escape this situation, I leapt to the floor trying to hide myself from his prying eyes.

Please don't see me.

Please don't see me. "You okay down there, lassie?"

Oh, fuck it.

I looked up and saw Mark standing over me.

"Yes, all good," I said, trying to wipe the last second of embarrassment from my memory and the coffee that was dripping down my chin.

"Was just looking for my dignity, which I seemed to have lost a long time ago," a chuckle escaped his mouth. I'm glad I can make someone laugh.

"Out on your early morning run, I see. I thought only losers like me are up at this time," I awkwardly laughed, trying to change the subject as swiftly and quickly as possible.

"Yeah I am, do you like running?" Mark asked, folding his arms.

"Yes," quickly escaped my mouth.

Correction, *no,* I don't like run.

The only running you'll see me doing is in the unlucky event of a zombie apocalypse.

"Oh, that's awesome you wanna join me tomorrow morning?" he asked, wiping the sweat from his face.

"Sure, why not, I was gonna go to the gym but a run sounds so much better," I said lying through my teeth.

What the fuck was I thinking?

"Oh great. I'll meet you here, let's say 6am?" he asked whilst looking at his watch with a smile on his face showing his white teeth.

SIX? WHAT THE FUCK!

"That's perfect." I smiled.

Now if the ground could just swallow me up that would be great. "Cool well I'll see you later," he waved running off.

I heard a giggle come from behind the curtain.

"How much did you hear?" I asked.

"Every single word," Iris said, laughing appearing from the curtain.

"Oh God," I mumbled, letting my head full into my free hand.

"You don't run…actually I haven't seen you run since…" She stopped to think.

"No, actually, I don't think I've ever seen you run," she said, sipping her tea with amusement.

"Very funny," I said with a nervous laugh. God, I'm such an idiot.

***

"Are you ready?" Iris shouted, knocking on my door.

"I'll be in five more minutes," I replied, looking in the mirror.

Studying my reflection for the tenth time this morning. I chose a swimsuit today that was Dalmatian print. Which sucked in all the right places and surprisingly made me look like I had boobs.

I looked up at Iris in the doorway in her red strappy bikini and straw hat looking insanely, annoyingly amazing. If she wasn't such a nice person, I'd hate her.

Looking at her I walked back into my room and grabbed my long kimono.

"Now I'm ready," I said smiling.

We both placed our towels on the same beds as yesterday.

I saw Jack, Marcus and three other friends that must have joined yesterday evening. I wanted to make sure we were as far away as possible.

"You wanna drink?" I asked Iris. It was only ten and I was ready for a cocktail if that wasn't foreshadowing this holiday I'm not sure what was.

"Do you even have to ask?" I knew Iris would never say no.

I got into the queue for the bar. My eyes wandered towards the tall guy two people in front of me and it was Mark.

My heart fluttered and the butterflies made a tornado in my tummy.

I watched him turn around and look down at the queue.

I instantly looked up at the ceiling. Soon to realise how hard it was to make looking at the ceiling interesting. My eyes slowly wandered back to him and our eyes met.

He smiled down at me and waved.

He had a pair of ray bans resting on top of his head and a patterned navy shirt that had all the buttons undone. The shirt matched his plain navy swimming shorts and I just wanted to yank that shirt off and let my hands wander. He looked like he just jumped out a Hugo Boss catalogue.

Once I reached the top of the queue, I ordered two espressos (both for me) and two strawberry daiquiris. I went to get my purse out and the barman stopped me.

"No need. That man has already paid for your drinks." He pointed towards Mark.

"What?" I said in disbelief.

"Yeah, I know he's beautiful." the barman said, winking at me.

"Now don't just stand here go say thank you," he said, passing me the tray with our drinks.

I walked over to Mark who was putting sugars in the teas, coffees and mixing the hot liquids. "Hi," I said standing behind him, I waited, he didn't say anything, so I moved around him and I finally caught his gaze.

"Shit, oh my God you scared me," he said hand on his chest.

His very bare chest.

I need a cold shower.

"Yeah, I normally have that effect on guys," I said, not being able to stop the laugh coming out of my mouth.

"I came to say thank you for the drinks," I said, smiling, lifting the tray.

"So you thought to say thank you, you'd scare me." His hand went to his hip.

"Well, that wasn't my intention but it was kinda funny," I said, scrunching my nose.

"Well, you're more than welcome. I couldn't not buy a drink for my new running partner." He smiled.

Damn, that smile would make any girl's knees go weak.

Especially mine.

God Damn it Bellamy pull yourself together.

"I…well we appreciate it," I replied pointing to Iris who was talking to Scott.

Mark:

"I see my friend hasn't scared your friend off." I looked over at Scott who was talking to Iris who by the looks of things was falling for every word.

Smooth bastard.

"There's still time," Bellamy laughed.

"Strange question and you can say no," I assured her.

"Will I want to say no?" she asked.

"The boys and I are going for dinner at Alexandro's tonight and it's really cool because it turns into a bar and club that opens up to the beach. I was wondering if you and Iris would like to meet us there for a drink later?" I asked, feeling the palms of my hands getting clammy.

Why was I so nervous?

She was only a girl and trust me, I've asked a lot of girls out but Bellamy seems like the type not to be afraid to say '*no fuck off*'.

"We'd love to," she replied.

Thank God for that.

"Okay, awesome, I'll see you later," I said with a massive grin on my face.

"I'll look forward to it," she replied.

I couldn't help but watch her walk away, enjoying the view a little too much. My eyes slowly drifted from the top of her head to her feet. Jesus holy fucking Christ.

She has a beautiful, full, feminine body and I wanted to learn every curve like the back of my hand. I nearly fell out of my seat when I saw her last night at dinner.

I made my way slowly back to the boys, reluctant to take my arms eye off her.

"Did you ask her?" Scott asked, grabbing his coffee from the tray.

"She said she'll only come if you aren't there," I replied.

"You're a dick," was his only response.

"I'm aware," I grinned.

"Mark, did you get my peppermint tea?" William asked from his bed, he didn't even look up at me he just lay there like a dead fish catching the morning rays.

"Yes, your majesty," I replied, walking over to him and handing him his tea.

William came out as gay when we were 17, we were all playing FIFA at my house having a laugh and talking about girls. Bill was the first to notice he wasn't being himself and asked him what was wrong.

"I think I'm gay," was his only response.

"You think?" I replied.

"No, I'm defiantly gay," he said tears filling his eyes.

"That's like saying I think I'm ginger," Bill laughed.

Bill has a way of making anyone feel at ease. He also has extremely ginger hair.

"I'm just glad you're finally admitting it to yourself," Scott said.

"Listen, mate, we don't care, be gay, be bisexual, be blue or green we sometimes might not understand but we will always be by your side no matter who you choose to love," I said to him.

"Cheers to that," Bill said.

From that day on, William changed, in the best way possible. I think he changed all of us in some way. Last year, we even attended a pride event in London to celebrate him and the man he has become.

"So did she say yes?" Scott asked urging for the correct answer.

"Yes, they will be there," I said, shaking my head back to the present.

A couple of hours later, we ordered our lunch and I was stealing glances over at Bellamy every chance I got. She put her big headphones on and kept making these faces so whatever she was listening to was entertaining her and I was so desperate to know.

"Take a picture it will last longer," Scott said leaning over towards me.

"Oh, shut up," I replied, pushing him away from me.

"Right, I think it's time we got a round of beers in," Bill announced.

"Plus, I need to get in the shade, gingers like me don't last long in the sun." He stood up and walked to the bar.

Bellamy:

After a long day in the sun, I was desperate to get into the cold shower and let the water soothe my now burnt skin. I wrapped myself up in the thin white dressing gown that they supplied and headed into the lounge.

I took two glasses from the cupboard and poured red wine for me and white for Iris.

"Oh, thank you." I looked over at Iris also in her dressing gown, hair half curled.

"We've got about two hours till our reservations so do you wanna play a round of beer pong?" Iris asked and at that point, my phone rang.

"Hold that thought." I grabbed my phone not recognising the number. "Hello," I said in my phone voice.

"Hello, this is Jane Morez, I'm calling about…" the line broke up.

"Hello," I said down the phone. "Hello," I repeated myself.

It must be the connection, yesterday I tried to call Mum and the connection kept cutting out until I went by the reception.

"Go down to reception," Iris said, reading my mind.

"Okay, I'm gonna go now," I shouted back at her running out the door, luckily reception was only across the road.

"Fuck," I hissed, not realising I'm still in my robe looking down at my bare legs.

"Hello Bellamy," I heard a distant voice from my phone.

"Miss Morez. Hi. I'm so sorry the connection here is terrible." I ran closer to reception.

"Hello, Miss Edmonson, are you there?"

"Yes, hello, I'm so sorry," I said with my hand on my chest slightly out of breath.

Maybe I do need to start running.

"Yes, I'm calling to say we would love to offer you an interview for the apprenticeship role."

"Really, wow, thank you so much." My heart was still pounding out of my chest.

"You are more than welcome. We will email you with further information."

"Of course, thank you so much again." I hung up the phone and I couldn't help but jump with joy.

"Oh my, thank God!" I whispered looking up at the sky.

"Interrupting?" I heard behind me. I turned around in surprise to see Mark.

"Hi sorry I didn't see you there." I couldn't help but smile. I felt so happy.

His eyes slowly wandered from my face all the way down to my bare feet.

"Clearly," he chuckled, eyes coming back up to meet mine.

"Don't tell me you're wearing that for drinks tonight because I don't think that's very appropriate," Mark laughed.

"No, I'm not. I just got a very important call and the reception in our apartment is terrible so in the rush, I forgot to put clothes on and apparently shoes." I laughed looking down at my feet.

"Erm anyway," I said shaking my head.

"I'll see you later?"

"I am looking forward to it, Bellamy." A little giggle escaped my mouth, hearing him say my name.

"Okay bye." I waved and quickly walked back to the apartment.

***

"I don't recognise myself," I said to Iris, looking at my reflection.

My hair was loosely curled.

I looked beautiful.

I felt beautiful.

I wore a skater wrap dress that was white with colourful flowers scattered around; it fell just above my knees. I didn't know whether it was the tan or the two glasses of wine I had whilst getting ready, but I felt good.

"I think you look beautiful," Iris said, finishing off her makeup in my bathroom.

Iris wore a red skin-tight dress that tucked itself into every curve of her body and she looked sensational.

"Too much?" Iris asked, plumping up her boobs.

"For you? Never," I replied.

Chapter Six
Mark

We left the apartment and walked to Alexandro's, the heat was still unbearable at this time, with a mixture of the sun and nerves I was gonna sweat through this shirt in no time.

Our reservations were not for another half an hour so we waited by the air-conditioned bar.

"Four beers please," I asked the bartender.

"You men speak so weirdly I cannot understand," the bartender laughed.

She was a very pretty Portuguese woman who didn't look older enough to be serving us drinks.

"We are from Scotland," Scott shouted over the music.

"We all talk weirdly up there," Bill laughed.

"Especially this one." Bill pointed towards Scott.

"I see, I see," she replied.

"Ignore them, they are still going through puberty," William said, laughing and grabbing a pint for himself.

I couldn't help but look around to see if Bellamy was here yet. I didn't even know this woman, I shouldn't want to know this woman but I just couldn't help myself.

"She's not here yet," William said.

"Who?" I replied, acting clueless.

"Who?" William said mocking me.

"You know who," he said, looking up and down at me.

"What?" I asked.

"Don't get any ideas," William said.

"What on earth do you mean?"

"He's saying don't sleep with the lass." Scott walked between us both, leaving Bill talking to the bartender.

"I'm not going to sleep with her." I want to, yes, but I won't. I can't.

"I would." Scott shrugged.

"I'm not even gonna rise to that," I said to Scott as my only other reply would have been to punch him in the face.

"You've got too much going on Mark, that's all I'm saying, plus she's not really a one-night stand kind of girl," William said.

I looked at him with a confused frown.

"Iris, now she's the one for a one-night stand," William said.

"I don't want Iris," I said.

"I do," Scott admitted.

"What I'm saying is Bellamy isn't the girl you just sleep with, she's the girl you take on long walks along the beach, who you want to bring home to meet your mum. She is a sensitive woman, wears her heart on her sleeve, she will fall in love with you and that is not what you want right now." William finished.

"I agree." Bill appeared out of nowhere, I cleared my throat gulping my beer.

"As if I'm gonna take any advice of you three idiots."

Bellamy:

"I cannot believe you made me wear these stupid shoes." I moaned to Iris, she insisted I wear her wedges. They were very beautiful, they just didn't belong on my feet.

"Well, if you wore heels more than once a year then maybe you wouldn't be wobbling all over the place."

"Yeah, I know." I huffed, still trying to walk properly.

"Here we are," Iris said, pointing to the restaurant.

It had fairy lights and ivy climbing the walls. All-white furniture and dim lights. This restaurant looked like it belonged in the Maldives. It definitely has had a massive upgrade since I last saw it. The last time we visited Alexandro's was when my sister turned 21. It soon got closed down until someone came along, brought it and made it into what it is today.

"Hello ladies, table for two?" the lady asked.

"Yes please," I said, taking a look around trying to spot Mark.

"It's so beautiful here," Iris said, looking out towards the beach.

The sea was calming tonight and very tempting, I was never one for swimming in the ocean but looking out at the sea tonight made me want to jump straight in.

There were still families on the beach, all locals by the looks of it and it filled my heart with joy. I always loved this beach growing up, not so much during the day but at night time, being able to walk on the cool sand, hearing the waves crash and seeing the sky turn, blue, pink, orange and yellow until the sun finally set. I have so many memories here of my grandad and siblings eating waffles on the sand after dinner and running around without a care in the world.

Whenever Iris and I go out for food, we always order a starter, main and dessert. We don't half-arse our food, especially on nights out like this that probably contain a lot of alcohol. I can handle my drink, Iris on the other hand not so much so I try to fill her up with as many carbs as possible.

Our cocktails arrived alongside our starters.

I had Giant meatballs and Iris had garlic bread.

Our second main course consisted of Carbonara which was both our favourite meal.

"Oh, my God I'm so full," I said, touching my round belly.

"Shall we skip dessert?" Iris asked, sipping on her mojito.

"Excuse me, what?" I said in disbelief. "Absolutely fucking not." I continued.

"Oh, thank God, I've had my eye on this Nutella cheesecake," Iris said laughing.

We asked for the bill, when we started to see the waiters moving the tables and chairs presumably to make room for a dance floor. Once everything was set aside, they opened the bi-folding doors that led straight onto the beach.

Iris and I moved to the bar and ordered our drinks followed by two Sambuca shots. Which will be highly regretted in the morning.

Then I saw Mark, Scott, William and Bill walking towards the bar. He looked extremely handsome, which I suppose wasn't hard. All four of the men are handsome, you normally got one who wouldn't be as good looking as the rest but not these four. I bet they had the girls back in Scotland swooning all the time. Mark wore a blue shirt that was fully undone and a white t-shirt underneath, with cream shorts and white trainers.

"Iris," I heard Scott shout, waving us over and handing us both a jaeger bomb each.

"Thank you." Iris and I thanked in unison.

We all cheered, my eyes meeting Mark's. He smiled and downed his shot. Iris and I took ours followed by our Sambuca shots and I then went to my whiskey.

"Blimey lass, slow down," Scott said to me.

"Oh, she's fine, trust me," Iris said, looking like a proud parent.

I smiled and shrugged my shoulders.

"What can I say I'm good."

Yes, I am being smug but the one thing I have is that I can drink, apart from my personality I don't have much else to offer. Plus, I hated the fact most men think they can out drink women.

"You hear that Gentleman that sounds like a challenge to me. Mark, mate, we've got a big drinker over here." My heart raced just hearing his name.

"Is that so?" he walked through his mates and stood opposite me, folding his arms, then said, "I just can't imagine something so small could handle their drink or even out-drink me." Firstly, I wasn't small, I was 5'6.

My face screwed up into a ball of frustration.

"Just because you're stupidly tall and have freakishly nice muscles doesn't mean you can out-drink me," I said, copying his folded arm.

"Okay, fine, four vodkas," he said to the barman. I laughed.

"That's cute, make that six Sambucus," I said, turning my face to meet Marks.

The barmen lined the six Sambuca shots. Three more for me and three for him.

"Você tem um isqueiro, 1 canudo, tesoura e um punhado de grãos de café?" (Do you have a lighter, 1 straw, scissors and a handful of coffee beans?) I asked the barmen.

"What on earth did you just say?" Scott asked with a confused look on his face.

"I was asking for some supplies." Looking back at the barmen who was collecting the items.

"Obrigada." I smiled.

"I've been coming here my whole life and if there's one thing I've learnt it's how to do a Sambuca shot properly," I replied as I grabbed the objects from the bar.

"Just trust her," Iris demanded.

I placed three coffee beans in each glass, I cut the straws in half, giving Mark a half and keeping the other for myself. I carefully lit the Sambucus, thanking God for a windless night otherwise it would be difficult to get a blaze.

"Right, let them warm up for a second. Before you take a shot, I'll blow them out and we put our two straws together like this?"

I touched both the tops of our straws together.

"Got it?" I asked, looking at Mark's blank face.

"Fucking hell yeah alright," he said, looking slightly nervous.

Now I'm really feeling extremely smug.

I blew out the flames from the Sambuca and lifted my straw up to Marks.

"Boa saúde," (good health) I said, then placed the straw in the shots and sucked up the warm liquid.

Once I finished, I looked at Mark, who was looking at me with astonishment on his face.

"What?" I said looking over at Mark's two full shot glasses.

"Couldn't take all three?" I mocked.

"I didn't know you spoke Portuguese," he said.

"You don't really know me at all," I said shrugging my shoulders.

"Now, are you gonna drink those?" I asked, looking down at the two remaining shots. With still no response, I took the straw out of his hand and finished his two for him.

"You suck," I said, flopping my hand over my shoulder with Iris giving me a high-five.

"You have left me speechless," Mark said.

"It happens," I shrugged.

Which, for your information, it *never* happened.

Mark:

I can't remember the last time I was left speechless.

She just downed five Sambuca shots and didn't even flinch.

Over the next hour, we all started to get to know Bellamy and Iris, they are both very funny, intelligent and both breathtakingly beautiful. They went on to tell us they've been friends their whole lives and this was their first holiday together. Bellamy also went into a little bit of detail about how she knew Portugal so well and the language.

An hour in, I left the girls, William and Scott dancing whilst I went to get another drink.

"You alright mate?" I asked Bill who was looking very green.

"I don't think so," he laughed, Bill could never hold his drink.

I asked the bartender from earlier for a large glass of water for Bill and a beer for myself.

I looked back over to Bellamy and she was whispering something into Iris's ear, which didn't concern me until Iris frowned, gave her a hug and watched her walk towards the sand.

"Is she okay?" I walked over and shouted over the music.

"Yeah, she just needs some space." Iris shrugged as if I am meant to know what that means.

So I followed her.

She stopped on the beach, took her wedges off and sank into the sand.

"Mind if I join?" I asked looking down at her.

"Of course not." She smiled.

"Alcohol getting to you? I hope not because I need a running partner tomorrow," I laughed, joining her on the sand. I looked over to her hoping for a smile or laugh, but nothing.

"Something like that," she said, looking into the distance.

She closed her eyes and took a deep breath, opened her eyes up towards the sky and let the air leave her lungs.

"Penny for thought?" I nudged her.

"I'd have to charge a pound for one of mine," she said, looking towards me. She smiled but there was a hint of sadness in her eyes.

"So Bellamy, who are you?" I asked.

I was intrigued to get to know her even just a little bit of an insight and I'd take anything she was willing to give.

"That's an odd question," she said.

"I'm an odd guy." I shrugged.

"That makes a lot of sense." She smiled.

"Who am I?" she took a deep breath and turned to face me again.

"My full name is Bellamy Kate Edmondson. I am 26.

I love documentaries. I watch Christmas romance movies all year round. I have a dog waiting for me back at home. His name is Rover and the love of my life… Extremely nerdy, especially when it comes to marvel, I love my friends and family more than anything. I've been single for three years. I haven't had sex for three years. Two years ago, I spent 6 weeks in a psych ward, but I assure you I'm better now and I've never been in love" – she paused, caught her breath and then continued – "That Mark is who I am."

My eyes didn't leave hers as I listened to her talk. There were so many questions I wanted to ask but knew I shouldn't. There were so many things that I wanted to confess that I knew I shouldn't.

"Well, Bellamy Kate Edmonson, you have officially become the most interesting person I know," I confessed.

"What's your full name?" she asked.

"Mark Barnes," I replied, smiling.

Both our eyes locked and before I knew it our heads were gravitating towards each other. Just before our lips locked, I heard a scream.

"Bellamy!" Iris screamed from the bar and then ran over.

"Come on girl, you've been out here forever," Iris said looking at me and then Bellamy.

"I just ruined a moment didn't I?"

"It's fine, come on let's go," Bellamy said looking over at me as I held my hands out. "Thank you," she said as she let me pull her up from the sand.

"Ouch!" she groaned, limping on one foot.

"You okay?" I asked, it was only three weeks ago when I accidentally stood in the glass on this beach.

"Yeah, just these stupid shoes are killing my feet, the price you pay for trying to look pretty," she laughed, picking up her shoes and shaking the sand out.

"You definitely don't need to try," I whispered in her ear, she didn't reply but from the colour of her cheeks, she heard me.

Bellamy:

Iris and I walked back to our apartment not realising it was 2 o'clock in the morning.

"Ugh," I groaned.

"What's up?" Iris said.

"I forgot I've got a run tomorrow morning with Mark." A nervous laugh escaped her mouth.

"It's not funny," I said nudging Iris.

"No, you're right it's not, except it's 2 o'clock, you've got four hours until you're up again. Oh, and you do not run." I must admit Iris was right and I was extremely nervous.

Chapter Seven
Bellamy

Dragging myself out of my bed at 5:30, which was not my plan this morning but I had to open my big mouth and say yes to running with Mark.

What. An. Idiot.

Putting my messy hair up on top of my head, I brushed my teeth and thanked my past self for washing all my makeup off before going to bed last night.

I put on my gym outfit that I brought with me. Looking at myself in the mirror I huff and slipped on an old T-shirt. I decided to help my mental health. I will try and get to the gym at least three times this holiday just to keep myself happy and knowing I'm working out I won't feel as terrible when I stuff my face with food every day.

I heard a knock at the back patio door.

"Hey," I whispered, opening up the door to let Mark in.

"Let me just finish my coffee," I said, grabbing the mug from the counter.

Giving me a moment to look at him and damn I hated how good he looked, even at this time in the morning.

He was wearing basketball shorts, a grey plain t-shirt and a massive smile on his face.

"What are you so happy about?" I asked, gulping the last of the coffee.

"Oh nothing, just feeling good," he said smiling and shrugging his shoulders.

"Okay you weirdo, let's do this," I said placing the mug in the sink.

"What I was thinking is that we start off with a slow jog and then hopefully speed it up," he said smiling, clicking his fingers on his Apple Watch.

Oh God, we're really gonna do this.

"Yeah sure," I said with a thumbs up.

I don't even think we are a minute into this so-called jog and holy shit I'm dying. I tried so hard to stay calm but I think my heavy breathing may be giving me away. My right boob was hurting and I'm pretty sure I was going to have a heart attack.

After what felt like a lifetime, Mark stopped.

"Oh, thank God," I muttered to myself.

"What was that?" Mark asked, turning around.

"Oh nothing, just the view is so nice isn't it?" I smiled, waiting for him to turn around until I could lean over and try to catch my breath.

Mark:

"You're not a runner are you?" I asked. She wasn't even keeping it a secret, her heavy breathing and groans gave her away pretty early on.

"No, I'm not and I think I'm having a heart attack," she said in between breaths.

"But you're so fit," I stated and she was, I didn't even mean in a flirty way it was just a fact.

"I'm a weightlifter," she said.

73

"Not a runner." She sounded like she was finally getting her breath back.

"Ah, I see," I couldn't help but laugh.

Now that would explain the muscles and toned arms.

"What?" she said.

"Why did you agree to go on a run with me?" I asked.

"I have this thing where I don't think before I speak, it's very common," she laughed waving me off as her eyes searched the distance.

We stopped in the square, there were bars and restaurants all around, still closed. The only people that were up were us and the fishermen who were pulling in their boats onto the sand.

"What are you thinking about?" I asked.

"My dinner tonight, the restaurant is known for its cocktails and desserts." Out of all the things she could be thinking of, food was on her brain. I also couldn't help but notice that smile on her face.

Lord help me.

"Is that the one up the hill?"

"So you know it?" she turned straightaway.

"Haven't a clue I just guessed," I answered, which caused Bellamy to laugh.

It. Was. Glorious.

Bellamy:

"I want to show you somewhere." I turned towards Mark and gave him the biggest grin because I just knew he'd appreciate it as much as I. Plus I didn't want to end this encounter just yet.

I led him up a very steep hill. The hill sat to the left on the beach and had zigzag stairs carved into the rocks that led all the way up to the top. White buildings with colourful roofs were stacked up like dominos, one after the other. We started trudging up the stairs with the sun now getting hotter by the second.

My calves were starting to feel the burn. Doesn't matter how many times I've walked these stairs my body always screamed at me the whole way up. But when you reached the top, you would receive the most spectacular view of the horizon, a church and a playground which I used to play at when I was younger. I always planned on getting married by this church one day.

"Blimey." I heard Mark huff letting out a long heavy breath.

"So you can go on a run, but you can't walk up a hill?" I teased.

"That is not a normal hill," he said pointing down the hill.

"Those muscles are very deceiving, come on it's not far now."

We reached the top and I walked over to the entrance of the broad walk. Our walk turned into a very slow stroll as the fiery ball in the sky burned down on us.

To the left, there was a line of massive villas that sat neatly looking out at the ocean. One of these villas held a very big place in mine and my family's heart but that's a story for another time. When you looked to the right, there stood nothing but the big blue ocean, which was looking extremely choppy this morning as you can see the boats bobbing up and down wildly.

"Just down here." I pointed down a flight of stairs that led to a restaurant in the cliffs, but if you took the turn to the left you reached the edge of the cliffs. Which was exactly where we were heading.

I walked towards an opening in the rocks.

"It says no entry." Mark stopped.

"Yeah, don't worry about that, it's been saying that for the past 20 years, come." I grabbed his hand and led him through.

"Are you gonna kill me?" Mark whispered.

"Not today," I replied. Mark stopped walking.

"I'm only joking, come on," I laughed, dragging him along. A few more steps and we will be there.

"Wow," was the only word he spoke.

I felt the wow myself every time.

Once the light appeared, it opened up to two holes that have been carved in the rock, which gave you the most spectacular view of the open ocean.

There was no end in sight. Just blueness.

Just one look down and you'll be able to see the waves crash against the rocks.

"I always feel so close to my family when I'm here. We spread my granddad's ashes here when he passed away 17 years ago." I looked over to him, but he was already looking at me.

It could be the tanned skin or the sunshine that was currently highlighting the blue in his eye. But I then noticed there was a small scar at the top of his left, dark eyebrow. His unshaven jawline was sculpted and his bottom lip was fuller than the top.

"What?" I chuckled nervously.

"Nothing," he said, poking his head out of one of the holes.

"What are they doing?" Mark asked, looking over at the men cliff jumping.

"I'll show you." I grabbed his hand and pulled him out of the cave towards an uneven, bumpy pathway, walking him towards the men.

"Daniel!" I shouted waving my hand.

"Bellamy." I heard being called back.

"Vê isto," (Watch this) Daniel shouted back before he back flipped off the cliff.

"Wow!" Mark's mouth gaped open.

"I know right." I smiled.

I have known Daniel ever since I was a baby.

His mother always hoped we'd end up together, always joking saying I was her English daughter-in-law.

"Ola," Daniel said, appearing from under the rocks.

"That was impressive," I said as we traded two kisses.

"Has Ma and Pa seen you yet?" He asked

"No, not yet, I'll try to go over there today and reserve a table for tonight." Daniel's eyes were light green and with his dark skin, it was impossible to look away.

He stood at about 6ft, had dark short hair and he was very slim. He'd always been skinny even when we were children.

"This is my friend Mark," I said, turning to him.

"Nice to meet you," Daniel said shaking his hand.

"I don't know how you did it," Mark replied, looking up at the top of the cliffs.

"Oh, that was nothing, this lady." His head nodded towards me.

"Jumped off that one over there a couple of years ago." He pointed to the higher cliff edge. "It took a lot of convincing," Daniel then laughed.

"That it did," I confessed.

"Anyway, we best be off but don't tell your parents I'm here yet I'll surprise them at the restaurant."

"Of course, of course, Adios." Daniel gave me a quick hug and then walked over back to his friends.

"How long have you known him?" Mark asked.

"Since I was a baby." I looked up at Mark.

"Do you and the guys want to meet with me and Iris tonight at a karaoke bar?"

"We'd love that."

"Oh good, that's good," I said with a giddy, big smile on my face.

You'd think this was my first ever encounter with the opposite sex with the way I'm acting. But it wasn't, I assure you.

Firstly, there was my first ever boyfriend Mathew. I met him when I was 18. He was a car salesman. He was on the short side, had brown hair, hazel eyes and tattoos everywhere. He had cauliflower ears from boxing and started a lot of fights when he was younger, which I suppose is what happens when you have a temper like his.

He was the first real man to take any interest in me. For a while, I believed him when he said I'd never do better than him. I've never been scared of people but he scared me. I remember I was up in his bathroom having a panic attack as I came out and sat on his bed still sobbing from my episode. He said he wished he was able to sleep so he didn't have to deal with my shit. It took me a while for me to realise how horrible he was. I cried myself to sleep so many times but luckily we soon ended after I caught him texting another woman.

Then there was Archie. Who showed me what true forbidden love looked and felt like. I met him when I just broke up with Mathew at a casino and he never left my mind. I found out he had a girlfriend after Iris Facebook stalked him. He messaged me one day over Instagram and from there we spoke every day. Time passed and our friendship turned into something else. What that was I'm still not sure but I knew it in my heart even to this day we were meant to be something. He would come to me about his family problems and I always asked why he did not go to her? His simple reply was that:

'She would never understand.'

The last time I saw him still wanders in my mind. He said to me he wanted to be with me and not her. I told him I felt the same. When we departed I went to message him on Instagram to find I was blocked, then to his Facebook and I was blocked.

After two weeks of wondering, I found he proposed to her.

Lastly, there was Jack.

The boy truly stole my heart and broke it just as quickly.

I met him at the gym. We spent two weeks constantly looking at one another. I finally plucked up the courage and smiled at him. The rest was history.

So here is how it ended. He just stopped talking to me. It was as simple as that. Until a week later he picked me up and told me, '*I don't want to be in a relationship anymore I can't do it. I need to be single,*' then two weeks later he was going out with Brooke.

Thinking about it now. I never loved any of them. I thought I did but I know I didn't.

Do people actually fall in love anymore?

I don't have a clue what love was when it came to men. I knew I loved my family, I love Iris. I would die for any of them but when it comes to men, I just don't think it's possible not in this day and age.

"You alright?" Mark nudged me.

"Yeah, I'm okay sorry I just got lost there for a moment," I said smiling.

"Do you do that a lot?"

"Do what?" I looked up at him confused.

"Just disappear somewhere in there," he said, pointing to his head.

I laughed, looked down and fiddled with my fingers.

"Probably too much," I replied honestly.

"Your freckles," he said softly, his hand reaching over to touch my cheek.

"Oh God," I said, automatically putting my hands over my face.

My freckles always made me self-conscious. I go from being a 26-year-old to a 6-year-old.

"Don't do that," he said, my hands slowly coming off my face to look up at him.

"Don't hide your face, you are beautiful."

Silence filled the air as we both just stood there looking at each other. His hand came up and cupped my face, his eyes travelled to my lips, to my eyes and then back to my lips.

Then it happened, our lips gently touched.

His lips left mine as quickly as they arrived, his other hand cupped the other side of my face and the kiss deepened, it turned into something with passion and hunger. His warm tongue traced my mouth, I was completely and utterly under his spell. He pulled away, almost in regret but I wasn't too sure. His hand fell from my face immediately, returning to his side.

"Wow." I couldn't help but smile, my thumb traced my bottom lip, not wanting to forget the feel of his lips on mine.

"Let's get you back to the apartment," Mark said before walking me back to the porch doors of the apartment. The walk back was quiet, both of us not really knowing what to say. I was feeling strangely content and at ease in his presence as if I have done this with him many times before.

Chapter Eight
Mark

"You've been gone bloody ages!" Scott shouted from the bathroom.

"I got distracted," I shouted back.

The door unlocked and Scott walked through.

"She's not your usual type," he said closing the bathroom door behind him.

"No, she's not," and she really wasn't.

All my relationships with women I've slept with were all petite, brown hair normally, slim and very timid.

But Bellamy...

She has beautiful blonde hair, freckles that spread across her face, she was a curvier woman, which didn't bother me. Her legs were full and muscly. You could tell she works out a lot. She looked like a woman men would never approach; she was loud, sarcastic and had a terrible potty mouth. She was unapologetically herself and that was the most attractive thing of all.

Bellamy:

Iris and I slowly walked down to the pool and I couldn't help but feel anxious to see Mark again.

After that insane, stomach-clenching kiss, how do I act?

I decided on wearing my boob tube swimsuit that was baby pink across the top, black at the bottom with a white bow that tied around my waist.

"BELLAMY." I heard Mark shout from the pool. He rose up from the sun lounger and stalked his way towards us.

Holy mother of Jesus.

There wasn't a lot of softness to his body. He was lean and defined but not big like a bodybuilder. There was a slight bit of hair on his chest. He looked like a man, he was a man, a strong man. My eyes then fell past his broad shoulders, down past his firm torso and then I felt a nudge on my arm.

"Stop drooling," Iris whispered as my eyes and mind came back to reality.

"Hi." I smiled, lifting my hand to stop the bright sun from blinding me.

"We saved two beds for you both if you wanna join?" he said pointing to his friends.

"Oh yes please," Iris responded instantly walking past Mark and sitting next to Scott.

"Good morning, Bellamy, I must say I've never seen anyone take shots the way you did last night," Scott said.

"Why thank you, it's something I'm very proud of," I beamed placing myself on the sun bed next to Mark's.

"I was impressed, never seen a lass do that and be able to walk at the end of the night," Bill spoke up. Bill was the shortest out of the lot standing just under 6ft whereas the others stood over 6ft. He had red warm hair that was styled in a topknot and had tattoos covering every inch of his body.

"I think you're just jealous she out-drank you, Bill," Mark laughed.

"Fuck off," he replied.

"Anyone can out-drink, Bill," William laughed.

"Don't be too sure on that," Iris said warning them.

***

A few hours passed and the sun was beaming down on us nearly reaching 40 degrees.

I think it's time for the pool I thought as I dragged myself up from the bed, feeling the sweat drip down my back. I took my first two steps onto the stairs letting the cold-water flow over my feet. Letting out a silent squeak.

"Is it cold?" Iris shouted over.

"Yeah but it's lovely," I replied, sucking in as the cold water hit my skin. I decided to brave it and dove under the water. I surfaced using both my hands to wash the water from my face and pressed the chlorine from my hair. I swam back up and walked out of the pool.

"Coming back already?" Mark asked.

"You see, I have a routine, get too hot, jump in the pool to cool down, then get back on the bed and let the sun dry me," I said using the towel to pat myself dry before laying it out and plopping my damp bum on the bed.

"Smart," Mark said as he put his sunglasses over his eyes.

"What are you listening to?" Mark then asked before I could get my headphones back on.

"A serial killer book," I simply replied.

"Sorry what?" he asked.

"A serial killer book, it's 20 hours long." I smiled. "It's all about the world's most notorious serial killers," I continued.

"She's a weirdo. It's either that, cults, ghost hunters, eighteenth-century romance or Marvel fan fiction," Iris smiled over at me.

Best friend, my arse.

"Girl, you need Jesus." William piped up still lying on his back.

"Nope I just need a drink," I replied lifting myself up off the bed.

"Anyone wants anything?"

"Holy water," William replied.

I looked over at William and raised my eyebrows and took my purse out of my bag, flipping him the finger.

"I'll pray for you!" he shouted after me.

"Please don't," I replied walking towards the bar.

I ordered a round of beers, a gin for Iris and a large whiskey with ice for me.

Later that day – Bellamy:

This is my favourite part of the holiday, waking up from a long nap, having a refreshing cold shower, being able to wash away all the chlorine from my hair and getting ready to go out.

Tonight's look was very simple: white culottes and a green crop top. I wore my hair in a low bun and only applied eyeliner, mascara, blush and highlighter.

"You ready?" Iris banged on the door.

"Yeah, coming," I said, grabbing my bag.

"I mentioned to Mark about this karaoke bar down the road I said we can meet them there at ten."

I said closing the door behind me.

"Oh my God yes," Iris said, clapping her hands.

"You got the key?" I asked.

"All here," Iris said, patting her bag.

We walked to the restaurant, which was a 20-minute walk from the apartment.

I couldn't seem to wipe this smile off my face this evening.

"So you and Mark?" Iris asked, raising her eyebrows.

"I highly doubt it," I said, knowing where she was going with this conversation.

"I see the way you two look at each other."

"Don't." I stopped her.

"The other one isn't bad either," Iris said slightly changing the subject.

"Scott?" I asked.

"Yeah, we actually spoke last night a bit and he's a really nice guy."

I looked over to Iris and she was smiling with rosy cheeks, oh my goodness she was blushing.

"What?" Iris demand.

"Oh nothing, I just haven't seen you blush in a very long time," I said shrugging off the comment.

"Shut up!" Iris spat, cheeks still rosy.

We both got seated at the end of the restaurant.

We weren't able to come to book reservations so we were very lucky to be able to get a table at this time. The restaurant was buzzing with activity. As we were seated outside, we were able to watch people walk by and slowly watch the world go around.

"What are you thinking?" Iris asked turning to face me.

"We only have three days left of this holiday and I'm afraid that I don't want to go back," I confessed with a heavy sigh.

"We always have to go back home," Iris laughed.

"I'm not worried about coming back home. I'm worried about losing myself. I feel like I've let go of a lot of anxiety and pressure that I put on myself," I said honestly.

"And you won't," Iris tried to assure me.

"How do you know?" I pleaded.

"Because I know you, Bell, I've known you and loved you through everything and I know if you really mean this, that you don't want to go back to the old you, you will not, no matter what it takes." She smiled and raised her glass.

"Here's to never going back." I smiled letting the late warm my face.

I have remembered this whole menu ever since I was eight. I didn't even need to look at it anymore to know what I wanted. Their shrimps in mouth-watering garlic butter. There was not one thing on this menu I did not like.

"Bellamy," I heard a man's voice come from the bar.

"Pablo," I said with a huge smile. I got up from my chair and gave him a big hug and a kiss.

"I thought it was you, I hardly recognise you without your parents," he said looking over at Iris.

"This is my best friend." I smiled at Iris.

"Hello." Iris smiled and Pablo gave her a kiss on each cheek.

"I saw Daniel by the cliffs this morning," I said.

"He did not tell us he saw you." Pablo shook his head.

"Where's Maria?" I asked, looking for Pablo's wife.

"In the hospital, drama, drama." Pablo shook his hand in the air, I could tell it was a topic he didn't want to talk about.

"I will let her know you stopped by, she will be saddened to know she missed you. Have you ordered starters yet?" he asked.

"No." I shocked my head.

"Trust me?" he asked.

"Always," I assured him.

"I will surprise you." He smiled.

"Obrigada." I smiled.

Pablo walked off straight into the kitchen.

He has owned this restaurant for nearly 25 years and my family loved coming here.

He walked around the restaurant like a headless chicken writing down people's orders and making sure everyone was happy. He worked so hard to make this restaurant a success, the food was amazing but the staff here made the experience even better.

My grandparents knew his uncle and auntie who own another restaurant down the road.

I remember when we returned the year after my grandad passed. We had to explain to them what happened and they were devastated. They made lifelong friends with my grandparents and the next generation (Pablo) was lifelong friends with my parents and I hope to have that with Daniel.

Not long after Pablo walked away, he returned with a huge steaming bowl and a large pouring jug full of red liquid.

"Octopus, caught this morning," he said proudly, as the bowl passed my face the smell reached my nose.

"Wow." Iris looked at the dish inhaling the smell.

"Please enjoy and this on the house." He placed the large jug on the table.

"Just a little something I put together for you both." Iris and I both beamed with joy and happiness.

I could tell by Iris's face she was starting to understand my love for this place and the people.

"Thank you so much, Pablo." I smiled.

"Yes, thank you, this looks amazing," Iris said.

Pablo nodded, smiled and departed back into the kitchen.

Once we got the bill, Pablo walked out with three large flaming Sambuca shots.

He handed me and Iris straws, I knew what was coming.

"Boa saúde para vocês dois." (Good health to both of you)

He smiled, then we all crossed our straws, blew out the flames and then sucked up the liquid.

"Oh, my God!" Iris screeched.

"Good?" Pablo asked.

"Extremely." Iris smiled back.

We both said our goodbyes. I hugged Pablo, promising him that my family and I will come back very soon.

We turned up at the karaoke bar just before ten and not to my surprise it was packed.

I looked around and all I saw were happy faces. Family's sitting at tables all making memories, parents laughing with their children, a huge group of girls, from what I could see one lady was wearing a sash declaring that she was the bride to be.

I couldn't help but search the crowds for him and then just like magic he appeared next to me with his friends.

"Hey." Mark smiled.

Here came the butterflies.

His arm wrapped around my waist and he kissed me on the cheek.

"Hey." I smiled, my cheek still burning from that innocent kiss.

"Hello, Bellamy." I heard a man's voice behind me and I knew exactly who it was.

"Olá Marco, tudo bem?" I asked (Hello Marco, how are you).

I'm not amazing at Portuguese but I can definitely keep up a conversation or try to.

Marco has been the owner of this bar for many, many years. He's been good friends with my dad ever since my dad rapped the whole of 'rapper delight' on the first karaoke night. They got drunk together and ended up waking up on the beach then the rest was history.

"Muito, muito bem, você parece tão crescido onde estão seus pais?" (Very, very well, you look so grown up where are your parents?)

Marco talked very fast so I found it hard to understand him, especially with all the music but I could pick out most of the words.

"Aqui sozinho com alguns amigos," (here on my own with some friends) I replied, looking over at the boys and Iris.

"Oh well, I must speak English now then," he laughed.

"How many of you are there?" he asked counting us all.

"Okay, you all sit here and I will sort this out for you." He led us to the last empty table.

"Thank you so much," I said with a grin on my face.

Mark:

This woman. I don't know what it was about a woman who could speak another language and look so natural doing it. I'm gonna need a very long cold shower soon.

A few minutes later, Marco returned.

"Here you all are." He was followed by two Portuguese waiters who were holding multiple pints and a tray of shots.

"Oh, you are a wonderful man," Bellamy beamed.

"I have my moments," Marco replied.

"Please put on my tab," Bellamy demanded.

"No, this one is on the house." He shook his hand.

"Muito obrigado Marco, me ajudando a impressionar meus novos amigos," Bellamy said.

I had no idea what they were saying. My eyes were just darting to and from them like a game of tennis.

"Alguns novos amigos muito atraentes, vou contar aos seus pais," Marco replied causing Bellamy to laugh.

I'm still completely lost.

"Vejo você mais tarde, Bellamy," he continued.

"Tchau," she replied.

Now that word I did know.

"Remind me to come to Portugal with you next time," Bill laughed smiling at Bellamy.

"Yes, this really is all amazing," William said, taking a beer from the tray.

I looked over at Bellamy who gave me a huge grin and touched my thigh. Which sent an electrical spark all the way to my heart and crotch. Her hand only stayed there for a split second and I don't think she knew what that action did to me.

Marco walked up to the mic and everyone erupted into a cheer.

"WOOOO!" Bellamy shouted and clapped.

"Welcome to karaoke night everyone," Marco spoke on the mic.

"We already have a huge list of people and we cannot wait to hear them sing. So firstly please welcome William onto the stage." Marco clapped.

We all immediately looked over to William who was getting up from his chair.

"Oh my God," Iris laughed.

"I love karaoke," William laughed, shrugging his shoulders, he took his shot and walked onto the small stage that was set up in the corner of the room.

The bar was decorated in all brown wood that lay across the ceiling, walls and floor, with old pictures of Portuguese musicians, along with the odd pictures of Elvis, Dolly Parton, Johnny Cash and many more.

As soon as William started singing, *Sweet Caroline*, the whole bar exploded in song, even I sang along. I kept looking over at Bellamy who looked so beautiful.

She wore white trousers that stopped mid-calf and they shaped her body to perfection when she walked to the toilets with Iris I couldn't help but look over at her, letting my eyes wander to her bum.

Wow!

I looked back towards Bill and Scott who were also doing the same thing.

"Hey," I said, hitting him on the head.

"What?" Scott said all innocently.

"Don't." I pointed towards both of them.

Ten minutes went by and the girls still hadn't returned so I looked over towards the bar and saw them both talking to a group of boys. Bellamy let out a huge laugh and touched the boy's shoulder. I shouldn't be jealous she wasn't mine and I can't see her ever being mine but I still didn't like it.

As she walked back to the table, her smile never faded.

"So, boys," Iris said, sitting back down on the stool.

"Bellamy's friend Daniel and his friends are inviting us to a sky bar later tonight if you're interested," Iris beamed and looked towards me and Scott.

Oh, Daniel, the guy who was jumping off the cliff earlier today. I didn't like him.

"Yes." Bill jumped at the chance.

"Of course." I smiled.

"Good," Bellamy said checking her watch.

"It's literally up the road from here, do you want to leave in about half an hour?" she said looking up at us.

"I'm so excited!" William cheered.

"Please tell me if there will be fit single Portuguese men there?"

He asked Bellamy.

"Why are you looking at me?" she asked.

"Well, you're the one that knows them," William said, his head nodding towards the men still at the bar.

"Well, Daniel definitely isn't, but I can ask," she said, raising her shoulders.

Daniel definitely wasn't?

How did she know?

Why do I care?

Definitely don't like Daniel.

Chapter Nine
Bellamy

Once we left the karaoke bar, Iris was extremely tipsy and asked Scott for a piggyback, which he was all too happy to give. Everyone was walking ahead of me and Mark, which I was pleased about because he has been acting rather strangely ever since I came back from the toilet and I couldn't help but want to know why.

"Are you alright?" I asked Mark.

"Absolutely." He smiled, grabbed my hand, twinning his fingers in mine as we walked up the road to meet everyone else. Such a simple gestor yet, I don't think I ever wanted to let go. This felt right, this felt... like it was meant to be. Or maybe I was talking utter bollocks and he just wanted to get in my pants.

You could hear the thumping of the music from down the road. I looked up and all I saw were flashing bright lights.

We planned to meet Daniel and his friends outside.

"Ola." Daniel smiled and gave me a hug, separating me and Mark.

"Ola." I smiled, exchanging smiles with the rest of the boys.

"Okay, let's go." His grin was wide, as he led us through the large, white double doors.

It was not what I expected. We walked in and it didn't look like a bar, it looked like a hotel.

Daniel walked up to the lady behind the counter. She looked down at her list and led us up a flight of stairs that led to a lift once we all filed in Daniel pressed the 'SB' button.

Once the elevator doors opened, the music came blaring through, slamming against your ears.

"Oh my God," Iris and I said in unison.

"Amazing right?" Daniel smiled over at us.

The rooftop was turned into a bar/club. There was a glass fence that lined the roof showing off the amazing view of the ocean and cliffs that surrounded us. It was spectacular, breathtaking and I was here with my best friend and these amazing, friendly, funny men. What a holiday this turned out to be.

"My friends are over there, please have fun," Daniel said, kissing my cheek and walking over to the rest of his friends.

"Shall we go to the bar?" I asked Mark, looking over my shoulder up towards the man towering over me.

Mark:

The lights were bright and colourful, slowly changing to all the different colours of the rainbow.

There were huge palm trees spread around the floor space that was planted in large white pots.

I looked out of the crowd past the glass fence and watched the waves and cliff edge meet in sweet harmony. The bar was swarming with people, laughing, drinking, singing and dancing.

"Can we get three shots of Sambuca?" I asked the barman.

"No six, get six," Bellamy demanded kissing my cheek.

"Okay, six shots of Sambuca." I shook my head signalling six with my fingers. Her lips left a burn on my cheek that I couldn't seem to ignore, I wanted more.

"Thank you." She smiled.

"Are you sure?" I asked, my arm now wrapped around her side to keep her steady on her feet. She wasn't drunk to the point where she couldn't stand but because it was so busy everyone was crammed together trying to get a drink and I wanted this woman as close to me as possibly. One to keep her safe and two for the most selfish reason of all.

"Trust me, I got this," she assured me.

"Alright okay," I admit defeat lifting up my hands in surrender.

The Barman poured out six Sambucas. I moved three over to Bellamy and left three for me.

"Alright, God I hate Sambuca." I cringed at the thought of these upcoming shots.

"Yeah but you don't hate me," she said in my ear, I turned to her and she had already finished her second shot.

"Down it, Mr Barnes," she ordered.

"Yes, ma'am," I replied.

How on earth I managed to get through those three shots without gagging I'll never know.

"The shit I do," I said still trying to recover from the aftertaste. Fucking awful.

"Has anyone told you how beautiful you are?" Bellamy said looking up at me.

"Beautiful?" I questioned, with a puzzled look on my face.

"Hell yeah, you're beautiful Mr Barnes." She smiled, her hands cupping my face.

"How drunk are you?" I asked.

"I am perfectly, perfect thank you very much." I don't know if she was trying to convince me or herself.

"I'm just appreciating the man standing in front of me."

"Okay, but beautiful?"

"Beautiful like a fairy."

"You're so weird," I said whilst looking around for the toilets.

"I'm gonna go to the toilet okay, you stay here." My hands on her shoulders looking deep into her eyes. I turned to see Scott kissing Iris.

"Scott!" I shouted grabbing his shoulder breaking their kiss.

"Make sure she doesn't flirt with anyone," I said to him then I faced Bellamy.

"I mean it." I pointed to her then I headed to the back of the club towards the toilets.

Bellamy:

Once Mark returned, I wrapped my arms around him and kissed him. Bold move Bellamy.

"What was that for?" he asked, his hand cupping my cheek, I hated this. I wanted more. The one simple kiss isn't enough, I wanted a lifetime worth of kissing in this single moment I want it all.

"You've got a very kissable face, Mr Barnes and I just can't help myself."

Iris and I danced most of the night together, having the best time, laughing and not caring who saw us.

"I'm so happy we did this." I tried to shout over the music.

"Me too," Iris said as she grabbed my face and kissed me on the cheek.

***

"Okay, good night boys!" Iris shouted from the porch door, waving and walking inside, bumping into the sofa with a little moan followed by *shit*.

"Good night Mark," I said kissing him on the cheek.

"Mmm no," he frowned, grabbing my hand and pulling me back.

"That's not how you say good night," he said as his lips slammed into mine, using his smooth, wet tongue to trace my mouth. Wow. That was... intense.

"Okay, good night," I said as my lips parted, blushing with the heat of that kiss.

"Boys." I nodded to Scott, William and Bill. Forgetting they were there for a second.

I locked the door behind me, noticing Iris asleep on the sofa she previously just bumped into.

I took my makeup off, brushed my teeth and got into my pyjamas. Checking my alarm for the gym tomorrow I noticed a message. I gave my number to Mark yesterday and I've been waiting for him to text me.

I can't stop thinking about you, and with that, my head hit the pillow and I fell asleep.

Mark:

I thought I would get myself to the gym early this morning.

I wasn't in the mood for running, and if I'm being completely honest, I was hoping Bellamy would be there.

I left Scott and Bill passed out on the sofa and William was in his bed.

98

"Good morning," I said to Maria who was always at the front desk during the week.

Her hair was black and always tied up in a bun that sat perfectly perched at the top of her head.

She had a scar that went across her left cheek, down to the end of her chin. Her smile was welcoming and no matter your mood, you couldn't help but smile back.

"Good morning, Mark, how are you this morning?" Maria smiled.

"I am very well, Maria, yourself?"

"Oh, very good; they say it will be very hot today so be careful," she warned.

"Yes, ma'am," I replied, smiling.

I walked into the gym and to my delight there Bellamy was in a crop top and black leggings, hair up in a high bun and she looked sweaty, hot and beautiful.

I looked over the gym floor and I saw some guys in the corner on their bikes.

It was lovely and quiet this time in the morning. The gym wasn't very big, the walls were all white, with ceiling to floor-length windows that looked out towards one of the pools.

Most of the machines were modern and new. It was very well looked after, always clean, always had music playing.

My eyes then moved back to Bellamy who has now moved onto shoulder press, lifting 16kg five benches away from me. I was very impressed. Not that I thought she was weak, she didn't have a weak body you could tell by the shape of her legs and shoulders she was strong.

Not that I spent most of my nights daydreaming about what it would be like to kiss her all over.

"Hey." I heard a man's voice from behind me, looking over next to me I noticed it was that guy Bellamy was talking to the other day.

I was so glad I didn't wear my headphones. I didn't want to miss this conversation.

"Do you need a spot?" he asked.

I couldn't help but think there was no way she would take any help and by the look on her face, she was pissed off.

"No thank you," she replied.

"Okay well, I was wondering…" I could tell he was nervous but before he could finish Bellamy dropped her weights, stood up and said,

"I'd rather fill my ears with shit than listen to you talk for another second."

A small laugh escaped my mouth. Very happy I didn't bring my headphones. This poor bloke.

This woman was brutal, fierce and even scared me. She put her headphones back on and carried on with her set. Her face scrunched up when the weights got too heavy, her face was red, damn she looked sexy.

"Found something funny?" I heard Bellamy next to me.

I turned to see her with her arms folded across her chest.

"I have no idea what you are talking about," I replied, acting clueless towards her attitude.

"Yeah I'm sure," she replied, frowned and then her smirk turned into a smile.

"You're an idiot," she continued.

"That's funny you're not the first person to call me that," I replied, she smiled rolling her eyes and swiping the sweat from her brow.

I loved making her smile.

"I'm sure I won't be the last," she commented before walked out of the gym, giving me one last look before exiting.

Bellamy:

"I just hate it, I hate him!" I spat out talking to Iris who was still in bed looking extremely hung-over.

"Why me?" I continued.

"I swear someone up there hates me." I pointed to the sky.

"God knows what I did in another life," I huffed.

"Do you need a spot?" I mocked Jack's annoying voice. "No, I bloody well do not." I folded my arms sitting on the end of her bed.

"Okay," Iris said, pulling herself out of bed, rubbing her temples. "Get up," she continued. I was trying not to hide my smile as her hair was perfectly resembling a bird's nest.

"Let's go to the beach today," Iris said.

"That way, we don't have to see Jack at the pool. Otherwise, I am bound to drown him," she said without even a hint of humour in her voice.

"Absolutely not, I hate the beach," I demanded, crushing her dreams.

"Really?" Iris moaned.

"Really," I said.

I hated the beach during the day. The sand was too hot to walk on, sand got stuck up in places where you didn't want sand, kids would run around spraying sand anywhere.

***

Within the hour we were both relaxing by the pool luckily for me Jack was nowhere to be seen, sadly for me neither was Mark.

"Drinks, ladies?" a server walked over with the list of cocktails.

"You know what," I said.

"We'll take one of each," I said, taking my purse from my bag. Two hours into our day we were five cocktails down.

"Oh my God," I said snorting, not be able to control my laughter.

"You remember that night?" Iris asked and yes I did.

It was my 20th birthday and we were both drunk.

I remember looking around and Iris was dancing with this guy who must have been at least 40 years old. I walked up to her trying to get her away, but she wouldn't take any notice of me until the next morning when she was texting this guy Lawrence.

"This guy is so nice," Iris said with a sore throat from all the screaming and singing.

"Who?" I asked.

"Lawrence," she replied.

"Who the fuck is Lawrence?" I asked.

"The guy I met last night," and then it hit me...

"Oh my God." I burst out laughing, reaching for my phone. I took a photo of them last night, for this exact reason.

"Oh my, I found it." I couldn't stop laughing.

"What?" Iris said looking confused.

I turned my phone to show her the picture.

"Lawrence, the lovely guy you met, yeah he's a 40-year-old."

"Fuck off," Iris said yanking the phone from my hand.

"Oh Jesus," she said covering her face.

"Jesus ain't gonna help you now," I laughed.

"Hey." Mark came over and sat down at the end of my sunbed. Making my heart skip a beat for the 10,000th time.

"Hey," I said, not helping but smiling. Still laughing from mine and Iris's previous conversation.

"Me and the boys are going to have a game of volleyball down on the beach in about an hour if you wanna join?" he said looking at both of us.

"Sounds perfect," I said.

"Grand see you then." Mark nodded his head, smiled and walked away.

"Thought you hate the beach," Iris said.

"Shut up!" I spat.

Mark:

Once the girls arrived, Bellamy took off her oversized tartan shirt and wrapped it around her waist and swept her long hair up into a bun.

"Okay, you losers, who's on my team?" she announced.

"Me!" Bill shouted.

"Who's on my team, then?" I asked.

Bellamy glared over at me.

"Me!" Iris shouted walking over to me.

I looked over at her shocked and so did Bellamy.

"I wanna be on the winning team," Iris continued, shrugging her shoulders.

"Right well, Scott, you're on my team," Bellamy insisted.

"That leaves me," William huffed.

"I feel like I'm reliving school all over again," he continued.

"How about we make things interesting," I said looking over at Bellamy.

"Go on then," she said challenging me.

"You lose, you go in the water, I lose I go in the water." I smiled I loved a competition and by the looks on Bellamy's face she wasn't going to lose without a fight.

"Deal!" she said, head held high as if she had a chance.

I won, obviously.

"I'm not going in there," she said.

"But you lost the game." I shrugged my shoulders. "So in you go," I said walking towards her.

Everyone started laughing.

"Don't!" she said pointing towards me.

"And you shut up!" she said towards Iris, Bill, Scott and William who immediately stopped laughing.

I was walking towards Bellamy. Who was slowly walking closer and closer towards the water.

"You're going in," I said to her until I noticed she was one-step away from the waves.

"No, I'm…AH!" she shrieked as her heels hit the cold water.

"Yeah, you are." I laughed and dragged her into the water with me.

"Mark!" she screamed and tumbled into the water.

As she raised from the water, detached.

"Oh my God," she continued laughing, she tried to swipe away the trays hair that were stuck to her face.

"Right," she said marching out the water and towards Iris.

"We're a team, yeah?" she laughed.

"Don't you dare!" Iris said running away, Bellamy ran after her catching her quickly and dragging her in the water.

"We go down, we go down together," Bellamy laughed.

I just stood there laughing with them not expecting to see Bill and Scott both then ran into the ocean to joined them.

"Coming in?" I looked over to William as I moved my arms to keep my afloat in the cool water.

"Saltwater isn't good for my hair," William said, "So no," he continued.

I swam over to meet Bellamy who was floating on her back. "Hey, loser."

"Hey, Barnes." She smiled and swam to meet me halfway.

I reached my arms out and pulled her towards me, she then wrapped her legs around my waist. "If these shorts are ruined because of the water, I'm going to drown you," she laughed wrapping her arms around my neck, I chuckled, I'd love to see her try. Her eyes were a light caramel colour, her eyelashes thick with water clinging to them. I could stare at her all day, counting the freckles that splattered across her skin.

***

Once we all got out of the water it was 4 o'clock so we decided to meet up for an early dinner at Alexandro's.

I got changed into dry clothes and waited for the guys outside.

"She leaves in two days." I heard Scott say walking up behind me.

"I know," I huffed.

"Are you gonna tell her?" he asked.

"No point." I shrugged.

"Not like I'm gonna see her again is it?" I continued.

"I just really like her, man," I then confessed.

"I know, it's one of those wrong times, right girl kinda moments." He shrugged.

Chapter Ten
Bellamy

"You and Mark looked pretty cosy in the water today," Iris said as she locked the doors behind us.

"I really like him," I confessed.

"Why don't you tell him, maybe you could try a long-distance thing," Iris shrugged.

"It won't work, he'll go back to Scotland and I'll go back to Essex. Plus, we all know how needy I can be."

"It's one of those right man wrong time kinda moments," Iris said wrapping her arm around my shoulder.

"Tell me about it," I said as my heart felt like it had just sunk towards the earth's crust.

Which is ridiculous.

I've only known him a couple of days and I feel this way…

But maybe, just maybe, fate has something in store for me that I'm just not ready to understand yet. Maybe I was meant to meet Mark for this exact reason.

He's helped me feel alive, helped me feel beautiful and for that, I am so grateful.

Mark:

After dinner, Bellamy told us she knew an amazing waffle and crepe place just up the road so we decided to have dessert on the beach.

"It's literally up here," she beamed. The sun was staring us down and you could see Iris' shoulders getting redder and redder.

She stopped in front of a small shop just halfway up the hill on the other side of the beach.

We queued up to go in and the shop was tiny. My car couldn't even fit in here.

"Blimey, it's tiny in here," Scott said. Both of our large frames took up too much room so I told William what we both wanted and we waited outside, plus it was like a bloody oven in there.

Iris walked out first with her waffle, followed by Bellamy with her Nutella and whipped cream crepe.

I could see the staff pouring the batter on the crepe machines and spinning them around, the waffles were also being made fresh, it all looked so delicious with all the topping lining three shelves at the back. Everything you could think of was there. The smell coming from the shop was intoxicating. If I could wrap this scent up in a bottle and take it home with me, I would. The sugary, chocolaty-like smell was heaven.

We walked over to the beach, planted ourselves into the sand and dug into our food. My Nutella filled crepe with bananas was googy, sweet and filling me up more and more with every single bite.

Looking out to the never-ending ocean. The big blue was buzzing with its dormant strength. The waves were crawling gently to the shore. The sand was cool and there was a gentle breeze that was blowing her hair behind her shoulders. I ached for more days like this, being in peace, the sun warming my skin and my friends around me.

Bellamy:

"I cannot believe tomorrow is our last day," I said to Iris as I handed her a coffee and walked towards the sofa with mine.

"I know but I've had the best time, Bell." Iris smiled. A knock at the porch doors interrupted us.

We both looked at each other.

"I don't know," Iris mumbled.

I frowned, lifting myself from the sofa walking towards the back doors. I pulled the blinds back and I saw Mark.

Not what I was expecting this morning.

"Good morning." I smiled.

"Want to come in?" I asked.

"Hi, Mark!" Iris shouted.

"No, it's okay I'm just going for a run…I want to take you out," Mark blurted out.

"On a date or with a gun?" I laughed.

"A date," Mark laughed his cheeks rushing a shade of red.

"Really?" I was shocked,.

"Yes," Mark replied.

"Really?" I asked again, just to make sure.

"Yes," Mark laughed.

"Are you really, really sure?" I asked just to be double extra sure.

"Yes, Mark, she will go on a date with you." Iris came and stood next to me.

"We'll see you later?" Iris smiled over at Mark.

"Smooth," Iris said as she shut the porch doors and sat back down with her coffee.

***

Laying down on the sunbed I closed my eyes. Feeling the heat beaming down on me, burning and toasting my skin. Sweat was dripping off my skin, causing my thigh to constantly rub together and it was getting sore.

I walked into the pool with Iris, feeling the cold water run over my skin. I ducked under the water.

"That's so nice." I smiled, pressing the water out of my hair.

I swam to the edge of the pool, leaned my arms against the side and rested my head on my arm. I closed my eyes again. It was so peaceful. I could hear the trickles of water that my legs were making as I slowly kicked. In the far distance, you could hear kids laughing and jumping in one of the family pools.

"Are you nervous for tonight?" Iris said, leaning up on the side to meet me.

Thinking about that for a second. I looked over at Mark who was laying down on the bed.

"Me? Nervous?" I laughed splashing her.

"What do you think?" I continued.

"Do you want to get out of here for a while?" I said looking over at Iris.

"What do you have in mind?" she said, raising her eyebrows.

20 minutes later, Iris and I were standing at the edge of a cliff.

"I can't believe you're making me do this," Iris said, bobbing in anticipation.

"It's perfectly safe, you're lucky we are not jumping off that one," I laughed pointing up at the cliff I saw Daniel jumping off.

"Well, isn't that kind?" she said, rolling her eyes.

"Are you ready?" I smiled and held onto her hand.

"If you're by my side, I'm ready for anything." Iris smiled squeezing my hand.

We leapt into the water, letting gravity send us down into the ice-cold blue water.

We both surfaced letting out a heavy breath.

"Oh, my God that was amazing." Iris smiled.

"I knew you'd love it," I replied.

I floated on my back letting the ocean move me in a calming motion.

The sea was just as terrifying as it was magnificent.

"I feel so free," Iris said swimming out towards the sea.

"It's because we are." I smiled closing my eyes.

"Looking out into the ocean makes me put my whole life into perspective," Iris said.

I swam to meet her, braving the deeper ocean.

"That's because when we are in something that is so big and vast we realise how small our troubles really are." I smiled, wiping the salt water off my face.

We swam over to the makeshift stairs that have been carved out in the cliffs and I helped Iris up. You had to wait for the right wave to bring you up to the steps. Otherwise, if you're too close to the steps when the wave comes then it will take you with it. I've done it once or twice myself. We sat up on the rocks and let the warm sun dry out our wet swimsuits.

We walked back to the apartment, talking and laughing. Then it hit me there was not a thing I would not do for Iris. She is my best friend, my soul mate. She will always have space in my heart that no man could ever penetrate.

"Okay, let's get you ready," Iris said as she followed me into my ensuite.

"You know I can shower on my own?" I suggested.

"Right, yes, of course, I'll get the Sambuca out." She turned around to look at me.

"To calm the nerves." She clarified.

"Yes, of course," I laughed, rolling my eyes.

Mark:

I knocked on the porch door feeling apprehensive of the night to come.

"Hey Romeo," Iris said opening the door.

"You're looking dapper," she said, looking at me up and down.

I wore my grey chino shorts and a white shirt. Scott made me wear a pair of his white boat shoes. I thought I looked like a right twat.

"Oh, thank you." I smiled.

"You look nervous," Iris said inviting me in.

"I am," I confessed with a nervous laugh.

"I just want to thank you," Iris said, handing me a glass full of wine, which I nearly downed in one gulp.

"For what?" I questioned.

"You've really made her smile," she confessed.

"So I just want to say thank you for being kind to her. It will mean more than you'll ever know." That was all she said before Bellamy walked out in a flowy light green patterned dress that fell to her calves. Her hair flew past her shoulders in a loose curl with one side tucked behind her ear.

"Too much." She smiled looking down at her outfit.

"You look beautiful," I said.

"Thank you." She let out a breath and smiled.

"Are you sure you don't mind, Iris?" she asked looking at her best friend who was already in her PJs drinking a cup of tea.

"Go have fun," she ordered.

"Be home by eleven!" she shouted as Bellamy closed the door behind her.

"I have a confession," she said.

"Go on…"

"I've had two shots already this evening," she laughed.

I gasped in shock.

"Having fun without me? I'm wounded, Miss Edmondson."

"No, I was so bloody nervous," she laughed, moving a stray hair out of her face.

"Can I be honest?" I said.

"Please," she replied.

"I had a couple of drinks already because I was nervous," I confessed.

We arrived at the restaurant which was located opposite the road to Alexandro's.

"Out of all the restaurants, I've never been to this one."

"Really?" I looked over at Bellamy shocked, out of all the years she's been here I was surprised to hear of a place she hasn't visited.

"Yeah, my parents have been, my sister and her husband and my brother and his wife. My mum said it was a couple's restaurant," she said.

"Not that I'm saying we are a couple." She assured me stumbling over her words.

"I'm just saying…oh God you know what just ignore me," she said zipping up her mouth.

We were seated outside, on the last row of tables, right next to the square, which sat in the middle of the restaurants and led straight onto the beach.

I looked over to Bellamy who was smiling, looking into the square watching kids dance to the music that was being played by a DJ. She then started to laugh at an old couple dancing with their grandchildren.

"I love it here so much, Mark," she said, looking back at me.

"I can see why."

"Can you?" she asked.

"Absolutely," I replied.

"That makes me so happy."

"Why?"

"Because this place means everything to me and my family and I love to know people appreciate it and see the beauty like we do. My sister got proposed to up there." Bellamy pointed to the church that sat on top of the cliff we walked up the other day.

"I actually have a picture of me and my siblings sitting on that wall with my grandparents when we were between 3–8 years old."

Her smile was bright, warm and full of nostalgia.

You could see the love in her eyes for this place and the memories it held.

"I'm sorry I can just talk about this place all day."

"Don't apologise I love hearing it," and I really did.

"Please tell me something about you," she begged while sipping her red wine.

"I have five siblings, six nieces and four nephews. My father died when I was ten and my mum did the most amazing job of raising us. I own my own gardening company. I love my job and I love what I do."

"A gardening business that's very interesting, my mum would love you."

"Really? Well, I am a very lovable person." I grinned.

"Yeah, yeah," Bellamy said, rolling her eyes.

We both ordered our meals and I was feeling so happy.

Our starters and mains were demolished and we both moved on to whiskey.

"Oh my God, I love this song." Bellamy smiled and I knew what I had to do.

"Come on then," I said getting up from my chair and giving her my hand.

"Are you mad?" she replied looking over at people who were sitting close by.

"Yes," I replied.

"Yes I am, now come on," I ordered and she took my hand hesitantly.

I dragged her to the middle of the square, my hand cupped her waist and I pulled her closer. *Sweetheart by Thomas Rhett*, rang through the speakers.

It was at this very moment I knew this would be our wedding song. I don't know how it will come about or when.

But I will marry this woman. She was the right woman. The hell with timing. I just somehow have to tell her about my current marital status, but that can wait. Now is not the right time.

"Nobody quite like you, sweetheart." I heard Bellamy singing along to the song. I pulled away and twirled her around, her laughter ringing through the air.

I'm pretty sure by now she could feel my heart beating through my shirt.

I was a man and I rarely got nervous, especially with women. I didn't get to 33 without my fair share of them but as clique as it sounded no one was quite like her.

Once the song ended, we unwillingly parted and I dramatically bowed.

"Thank you for that lovely dance."

"Oh, the pleasure is all mine." She nodded her head and we both laughed. "I knew you'd enjoy yourself," I said smugly walking back to the table.

"Oh, shut up," she said, shoving past me.

I couldn't help but smile.

Bellamy:

That had to be one of the most romantic, embarrassing things I have ever done and I loved every minute.

"Madam," one of the waiters, came over to our table with a large glass of red wine in hand. "The gentlemen at the bar said it was your favourite," at that point, she quickly placed the red wine on the table and walked away.

I turned towards the bar to see Jack and his friends.

Mark's eyes followed mine.

"I'm going to lose my shit!" he hissed.

116

"It's okay." I put my hand on his and raised from my chair with the red wine in hand.

"Where are you going?" he asked with panic on his face.

"I'm going to end this," I simply replied and stormed over to Jack and his friends.

"Did I get the wine wrong?" Jack laughed.

"Listen, you little shit" – I said slamming the wine on the bar drawing attention to myself – "Grow the fuck up. I've had enough of you and your bullshit. You broke me in more ways than I care to admit. I missed you for so long but what was I missing from a 28-year-old boy?" I looked at him up and down.

"I've healed from so much pain and I will not allow you to humiliate me. I deserve better and I have always deserved better. I am such a better person now but you will always be a bitter, jealous, narcissistic boy and I pity you. So if you don't mind I'm going to walk back to my table and sit down with that handsome man that is actually interested in me, so you can take this wine and choke on it." I turned to walk away.

"You were never fucking worth it anyway. Go back into the mental home," Jack muttered.

That's when I heard the chair Mark was sitting on moving across the floor.

I put my hand up to let Mark know I was okay and he sat back down slowly.

The one thing I didn't need right now was a fight going on between two men. I thought better of reacting therefore, I ignored his comment and walked towards Mark.

"Shame she isn't as slaggy as her best mate," Jack muttered and from that point, there was no turning back. My fist screwed up into a ball and all my anger came rushing towards his face.

"Say what you want about me but don't you dare speak of my best friend," I spat out in anger.

Looking at his friends I turned around, walked over to Mark.

"Shall we get the bill?"

Mark nodded, asked for the bill, we paid and then left very quickly.

I never turned around to see Jack and I didn't want to.

"Are you okay?" Mark asked, trying to keep up with my quick pace.

I walked straight onto the beach and I just carried on walking. "No, my hand really hurts," I said, shaking out my fingers.

I've never punched anyone before, but I'm kind of glad it was him.

"Hey," Mark said, stopping me, holding me by the shoulders.

"Let me see your hand." I placed my hand in his and he placed the gentlest kiss on my already bruising knuckle.

"That was really brave," he said.

"Yeah right," I chuckled.

"I just punched him," I said flaring my arms.

"Yeah well, if you weren't gonna do it, I was," I laughed and then snorted.

"What was that?" Mark asked.

"What was what?" I laughed, followed by another snort.

"That," he said pointing at me and we both laughed.

Mark's hand cupped my face and he leaned down and kissed me.

My arms came around his neck and I leaned up and carried on our kiss.

At this moment, a bright flame was just lit. Our tongues tangled and I wanted more.

His arms came around me and squeezed me tight.

"I don't want this to end," Mark said breaking our kiss.

"Me either," I admitted I just wanted him to take me there and then on the beach.

Mark walked me back to the porch doors at the apartment, we held hands the whole way talking about Mark's gardening company. He was a very smart, amazing man who built a successful company from nothing. No wonder he had the body he did.

Mark:

As we reached the back porch, I knew she'd ask me to come in and I knew I couldn't. "Do you want to come in?" she asked, her eyes filled with hope.

There it is.

"I better not, I've got to be up pretty early for a run," I lied.

"Oh okay, yeah don't worry about it, well I'll see you tomorrow," she said her head falling to the floor as she retreated into the apartment.

I couldn't leave her like this.

"Wait!" I said, pulling her back so she was close to me, I could smell the Hawaiian tropic on her skin.

"What?" she asked with a smile.

I couldn't help but kiss her.

I knew I couldn't have her in that way, but I still wanted her to know I needed her and ached for her. My lips slammed into her as my hands pulled her closer.

She tasted like sweet, rosy red wine.
I felt like I've been waiting for her forever.

Chapter Eleven
Bellamy

The last day was here and I ached to stay here forever. I felt more at home in Portugal than I did in England. I slipped on my khaki green two-piece, which was high-waisted.

I walked over to the mirror and I still couldn't see anything someone would want. It was so frustrating fighting with your mind every day.

This is my body.

I can't exchange it for a smaller, petite, bigger boobed, smaller waisted version.

I can go to the gym, lose weight, gain weight, get a tan, but this is still my body. These are my stretch marks, this is my cellulite.

"Iris, are you ready?" I shouted from my room.

"I'm already waiting," Iris shouted back. Now that surprised me.

We walked towards the pool and sat down on our usual beds and within ten minutes, Mark and his friends came to join us. Mark smelled like sunscreen and aftershave and looked like heaven.

Mouth-watering, vagina, aching heaven.

He was wearing his black ray bans, which matched his black swimming shorts and smooth tanned skin. His beard was now hiding his dimpled chin. He definitely looked sexier with fuller facial hair.

"Good morning." He smiled, taking off his glasses.

"It is, isn't it?" I beamed.

Mark:

Bellamy looked beautiful this morning in her khaki swimming suit. She was tanned, her freckles have now travelled to her shoulders and down her arms. Her swimming bottoms were lower than usual and showed some marks on her stomach, which didn't bother me at all. I loved looking and seeing new things about her, seeing what made her, her.

"Iris and I were thinking," Bellamy said.

"That's dangerous," Scott muttered.

Iris replied by punching him on the arm.

"I would have gone for the face," I said, which made Bellamy laugh.

"You are horrible." She shook her head.

"Sorry, ladies you were saying," Scott said rubbing his arm.

"We were WONDERING!" Bellamy shouted.

"If you and the boys wanted to come over before we all go out for dinner tonight?"

"We'd love to." Scott smiled.

I fell asleep with my hand on Bellamy's thigh. It was their last day here. I wanted to make sure I could spend as much time with her as possible.

"Good nap?" she whispered as I slowly opened my eyes and readjusted myself on the bed.

"Why are we whispering?" I whispered back.

Her head nodded to everyone else asleep on their beds.

"Ah," I whispered, lifting myself up from my bed. "Wanna go for a swim?"

"Always." She smiled.

"Holy shit balls, it's colder than yesterday." She sucked in a breath stepping down to the last step of the pool. So I did what many men would do and I splashed her.

"Mark Barnes!" she shrieked, wiping the water from her face.

I couldn't help but laugh as she splashed me back.

"Oh, shit it is cold," I said as the little drops of water hit my stomach.

"See," she laughed, splashing more water on me.

"Not so funny now, is it?" she smirked.

She slowly lowered herself into the water, leaning her head back into the cold blue liquid.

"You're so beautiful." I smiled at her, watching as her face screwed up into a ball.

"Shut up, Barnes," she said shaking her head.

"I've always wanted to travel to Scotland," she said leaning on the side of the pool.

"Oh, it's beautiful before my dad died he used to take me up to loch ness and we would go on these walks, we'd be out all day long from about seven in the morning to eight at night.

My mum used to get so angry with us because most of the time we'd get home muddy, wet and once the next day I had a terrible cold and I had to skip school and my mum was fuming." I loved talking about my dad, he was such an amazing man.

"How did he pass away? If you don't mind me asking," Bellamy said, still looking over at me.

"He took his own life." I simply answered.

Bellamy looked over me with sympathy written all over her face.

"Don't say it." I urged, she frowned at my request.

"Don't say I'm so sorry, or that's terrible." I hated that, once anyone knew about my dad or lack thereof a look of pity would cross over their face.

"Well, I'm sure he'd be extremely proud of the man you have become, he sounds like a really amazing man and a great dad." Bellamy smiled.

"He really was," I agreed. He was the best dad and gave me the best first 10 years of my life. We never knew he was struggling, he kept everything so close to his chest.

"How did you get that?" she said looking at the scar on my chest.

I could tell her the truth but that was a can of worms that didn't need to be opened.

"I was young and extremely dumb." I shrugged.

Once Bellamy and I came out of the pool, everyone slowly, one by one woke up from their naps.

"Nice sleep ladies?" Bellamy asked.

"Lovely." William smiled yawning.

"Drinks?" she announced, lifting herself up from her bed.

Bellamy:

I came back with everyone's drinks and I stubbed my toe on Mark's sunbed. "Oh, fuck me sideways!" I screamed.

"You have a way with words." Mark shook his head in disapproval.

"Yeah my mum's very proud," I muttered back, limping to my sunbed handing everyone their drinks.

"On other news, Bellamy, is it true that you get woken up every morning to the Avengers theme tune?" William asked.

My eyes darted straight to Iris.

This girl was in deep shit.

"Yes," I said proudly. "Yes, it is." I smiled.

"Geek," Iris coughed, causing Mark to chuckle.

"I'm not even ashamed," I said plopping down on the sunbed.

I'd rather be a passionate nerd than a non-passionate person.

I find that when people talk about a topic they love; you see a completely different side to them, their eyes will shine differently and their smiles will become brighter and wider, it's the most wonderfully beautiful characteristic to develop.

"Bellamy." I heard Jack's voice from behind me.

I turned over in shock, pulled my sunglasses down and got a good look at his black eye. What a welcomed sight.

"Yes?"

"Can I have a word?" he asked looking down at me.

"If you have to," I replied getting up off the sunbed.

I could see Mark in the corner of my eye, watching the exchange with gritted teeth.

I walked over to the bar with Jack and we both sat on the stools.

"I wanted to apologise," he said with his head down looking at his hands.

I nearly fell out of my seat hearing those words.

"I'm not a dick, Bellamy but that's all I've been towards you recently" – he looked at me – "I've done a lot of stupid things in my life, and letting you go was one of them, even how I treated you, it wasn't right and I'm sorry. You deserve nothing but happiness, Bellamy." He smiled. I felt all the anger and disappointment that I felt towards him vanish. I've always wanted closure and now I have it.

"Thank you, Jack," I said.

"Aren't you gonna apologise for punching me?" Jack questioned.

I thought about that for a second.

"No, you deserved it." I shrugged my shoulders, got off the barstool and walked back to the sunbed.

"What did he say?" Iris came over and sat on the edge of the bed.

"He apologised." I smiled.

"Fuck off, no he didn't," Iris said scrunching her face with disbelief.

"I know, I was shocked too," I admitted.

It was nice to not have to hold such a grudge against someone. I didn't want any more hatred and bitterness in my heart.

"He's still a dickhead," Iris muttered.

"I'll drink to that," Mark replied.

I looked at my watch and saw that it was 2 o'clock.

"Right, I'm gonna go for a nap," I said raising from the sunbed.

"Come to ours at about six?" I smiled looking at the boys who saluted me as I walked away leaving Iris sunbathing.

"Love you!" she shouted at me.

I opened up the door, walked over to my room and face planted my bed and let the cool breeze send me to sleep. I could smell the heat, mixed with sunscreen and chlorine.

The loud alarm clock woke me up. I rubbed my eyes as I pulled myself from the bed. I walked into the kitchen and poured Iris and myself a large glass of Rose from the fridge.

I walked over to Iris's room and I could hear her snoring from here.

"Rise and shine. It's our last night let's do this!" I shouted and shoved the wine glass in her face.

She took it slowly, eyes still closed and gulped it.

"Have a shower, and then we'll get ready together," I said walking out of her room.

I put country music on, full volume and had a refreshing cold shower. Singing to the songs as I rubbed my after-sun on bobbing away to the music until Iris came in and joined me.

Two hours later, we were both ready.

Iris wore a tight nude dress that barely covered her bum. She looked sensational.

Like always.

I wore a silk emerald green dress, the only dress I actually brought from my shopping trip with Alice. Iris helped me and wrapped my hair up in a low bun. I wanted to make an extra effort tonight so I also put more makeup on than usual.

Mark:

We walked over to the girl's apartment and I could hear Bellamy from here laughing with Iris. It automatically brought a huge grin to my face.

"Oh, you are so fucked," William said looking at me.

"Excuse me?" I said stopped walking and looked at him.

"Your royally fucked mate," Scott then said, patting my shoulder and walking on with the boys.

William just shrugged his shoulders and walked on.

I just stood there like an idiot. Fucked? Why was I fucked?

Then it hit me. I've fallen for her. The one girl I can't have. Not yet anyway.

"Sounds like we are missing out on all the fun," I said as I saw Bellamy and Iris taking shots, sitting at the table that was on their porch.

"That you have, Mr Barnes," Bellamy beamed.

She looked like a movie star. There was something different about her I couldn't quite put my finger on but that satin thin dress did things to me I wasn't proud of.

"We've been waiting for you," Iris laughed pointing towards the four Sambuca glasses.

"What a couple of lassies you are," Bill said sitting at the table, taking his shot.

"You've got a lot to catch up on." Bellamy smiled, like an innocent child.

Bellamy:

After two games of beer pong, which Iris and I lost, we made our way very slowly to the restaurant.

"No, mate, rugby isn't back on till September." Bill corrected Scott.

I then started to listen to their conversation.

"Without me, you're all probably gonna suck," Mark laughed. Without him?

"We might actually have a chance of winning this year without you getting in the way," Scott laughed and Mark smacked the top of his head in response.

"At least our rounds will be cheaper." William shrugged.

"Alright, Jesus sounds like you can't wait to get rid of me," Mark laughed.

I looked up to him, I always thought he'd be going back to Scotland.

"I'm going to Tokyo next week to visit my brother and then I'm moving to London for a while. I'm staying with my aunt," he said, looking down at me.

"Sounds like you're going on a little adventure." I forced a smile.

"Something like that," Mark said.

I got the feeling he didn't want to talk about it, so I didn't ask any more questions, even though my natural self was aching for answers.

We reached Alexandro's and the waiter was standing outside the doors looking through the bookings for the night.

"Hello," Scott said.

"Gentlemen and beautiful ladies, it's so nice to see you all again." The kind man smiled.

"You too, sir, we have a booking at eight," Mark said.

"Ah, I see, yes okay," he said looking through the list.

"This way," he turned on his heels and walked us to our table.

We all filed through the doors and walked through the restaurant. I saw families all sitting around the tables laughing and having fun. I have a new, growing love for this restaurant and I can't wait to bring the family here when we next come.

We all decided we'd spend our last night here at Alexandro's. Where it all began.

"Bell you coming?" Iris said.

"Sorry yeah," I laughed.

Walking over to the table I saw Mark pull out the chair next to him, he looked up and waved me over.

"Why thank you," I said sitting in the seat.

Once we all ordered our food and the drinks arrived, Scott raised from his seat and lifted his glass in the air.

"Now I must say girls, this holiday would not have been the same without you both, it's been an honour to get to know you, for us we have another few days here in paradise but we want to wish Mark the biggest farewell, we'll miss you, brother." Everyone cheered and glasses met each other all around the table.

I couldn't help but feel my heart drop.

I felt extremely jealous and hatred for the next girl who got to kiss those lips.

There was no real future with him as much as I could think or dream of it. It's just not realistic, he would go back to his life and I'd go back to mine.

"Oh my God!" Scott said as the waiter placed a round of shots on the table.

"Oh yes, now stop whining and drink," I replied handing him a shot.

"That's my girl," Iris said lifting a shot to her mouth.

"You're a psycho," William said. "But damn girl if I wasn't gay," he continued.

"Okay, okay," Mark said, "Enough," he continued.

William lifted his hands in defence.

Mark's hand then went onto my leg and made soft circles with his thumb, slowly going up my leg. Higher and higher…

"Do you want to go on a walk?" I asked.

"I could use some fresh air before dessert," Mark replied.

"You do realise we're sitting outside?" Scott shouted after us as we had already left the table.

Mark held my hand as we walked down towards the beach.

He pushed me up against a wall of rocks and planted the deepest kiss on my lips.

The way he kissed me was like he was starved of oxygen and the only air supply was my mouth.

I felt like I was sinking into him.

His arms came and wrapped around my waist and he squeezed.

"I'm crazy about you," Mark said in between breaths.

I looked into his eyes and I felt the same but after this night I am left with wanting a guy I can't have.

"I want you," Mark admitted and it surprised me for a second because I realised I wanted him too in every way possible.

As our lips came together again, our phones started to ring.

"God's sake," I muttered.

"Hello," we both said in unison.

"Bell, please come back Scott and Bill are having a fight!" Iris shouted down the phone.

"Wait what?" I heard Mark shout down his phone.

"Okay, we are coming." We both looked at each other and ran back to the restaurant, to what we saw looked like a boxing match.

"What the hell are you doing?" Mark shouted and ran in the middle of them both.

"Enough!" he shouted.

William came behind Mark and held Scott up who was bleeding from his eyebrow and lip whilst Mark held Bill up who was bleeding from his nose.

"Oh my God!" I heard Iris as I saw the blood on her arm.

"What happened?" I asked rushing over to her.

"I think it was the glass." She started to tear up, my eyes went straight onto the long cut on her arm.

"I can't leave you two idiots alone for five minutes." Mark was shouting he looked at me with guilt written all over his face.

"I've got to get Iris back," I said, folding three napkins around her cut.

We both just looked at each other and I mouthed 'I'm sorry' he just took a deep breath and nodded. Iris and I walked down the beach towards the apartments and I couldn't help but feel heavy.

That was the last time I'd see him. I looked back one more time to see Mark yelling at the boys. I waited to see if he'd look at me but he never did.

"I'm sorry," Iris whimpered.

"Don't be silly." I tried to assure her.

"No, I am I've never seen you this happy and I stole your last night with Mark."

"Listen, chicks over dicks always," I said, trying to convince myself I didn't care.

We took the walk back in silence, which I suppose we both may have needed.

"What happened anyway?" I asked whilst placing the key in the lock.

Flicking all the lights on and dragging Iris to the sink. I started cleaning her cut and Iris began to tell me the story.

"Honestly, I don't know we were all talking about girls and then Scott mentioned this girl and then Bill got angry and then they started yelling at each other, William tried to laugh everything off but they had so much to drink and they got angry real quick. Scott threw the first punch and it went on from there, really." She sobbed.

"Ah," Iris moaned, I apologised trying to make sure there wasn't any glass in her arm.

"I can't believe they had a fight over a girl." I shook my head looking through the cupboards for a medical box.

"They are in their 30s, for God's sake!" I spat out shaking my head in disapproval.

"Yes," I said, pulling out the medical box from under the sink and wrapping white gauze around her arm and sealing it with medical tape.

"Right there you go my lover, good as new."

"Thanks," Iris replied, popping the kettle on.

"I'm sorry," she said again.

"Listen, stop apologising, okay this isn't your fault, these things cannot be helped." I saw a tear fall down her cheek. I wrapped Iris up in my arms and we stood there for about five minutes just hugging each other.

Mark:

"You two are such idiots!" I shouted at Scott and Bill.

After I apologised to the staff and the restaurant manager, I gave them my number to call for any further charges for all the mess and broken glass.

I cannot believe I left her this way.

The look on her face when she left almost made my heart shatter.

Bloody stupid men, the lot of them, me included.

"Sorry Mark," Scott said, who was walking by my side.

"You're an idiot!" I spat back at him.

"We are both sorry," Scott continued, ignoring every word that came out of my mouth.

"Just why, you both had to ruin the night?" I stopped walking.

"You both are as bad as each other." God, I sounded like my father.

I thought about texting her but maybe it was better this way.

No awkward goodbyes, just a silent understanding.

She made me feel again and for that, I am so grateful.

Chapter Twelve
Six Months Later – Bellamy

I thought about Mark today. I even thought about calling him. I can go weeks without him entering my brain but since last night I couldn't escape him. Maybe deep down I'm hoping he hasn't moved on and he still thinks of me and what we could have been. If only we weren't worlds away.

"Oh Bellamy, please sit up, you're slouching." I heard my mum call from across the table.

"Sorry," I mumbled, straightening myself in my chair.

"Happy Sunday everyone!" Dad cheered, raising his glass of wine.

I looked over the table and saw my whole family, including Iris over for our traditional first roast of the year. Everyone was smiling, but most importantly they were happy.

My brother Alexander came home from Afghanistan two weeks ago and he wasn't going back for another three months so it was amazing having him home. Knowing he was safe meant everything.

"When are you girls back at the hospital?" Sarah asked looking over to Iris and I.

"I'm back tomorrow but then I have the next day off," I replied.

"I'm not back till next week," Iris beamed.

"Lucky Bitch," I muttered under my breath, giving Rover a piece of my chicken under the table.

"You better not be feeding that dog," Mum scolded.

"Yeah Bellamy," Alexander mocked. Thankfully, he was sitting opposite me so he received my foot in his shin.

***

"Good morning, girl," Taya said over the desk handing me a coffee.

"You know the way to my heart," I said, sipping the warm brown liquid.

Taya has been my rock since I started at the hospital. She has taught me so much, helped me with the best way to physically handle patients, she even secretly lets me sit down with her when she does blood tests and cannulas, not that I'm allowed to do them but I'm so eager to learn, I secretly think she just got fed up with me asking 100 questions every day.

"Have you heard anything back from the interview?" Taya asked downing the rest of her coffee, finishing off some paperwork.

I had my interview two months ago. It went really well, from what I could tell. I felt confident. I felt extremely hopeful. I just hope and pray I do well, it's taken me years to decide what I want to do and now I do, I just really want this opportunity to prove myself.

"Nothing yet, I'm so nervous," I confessed.

"You'll get it!" she said, patting my back. Lifting up to grab some paperwork over my head.

"Here, let me," I said, lifting up from my chair.

Taya stood at 5 ft 1 inch, she was naturally petite. People were naturally drawn to her as she was such a friendly person it was hard to not smile or feel a little bit happier once you saw or spoke to her.

"Thank you." She smiled.

"Anything for my favourite nurse," I beamed.

I got to do my rounds, talk to the patients and actually drink my tea whilst it was still hot. Which was a rarity in a hospital. I'm on a post-op ward today so my day will consist of emptying catheters, taking blood pressures, making beds and helping clean patients.

"Bellamy?" Sandy asked from her bed, who was currently recovering from a knee replacement.

"Yes?" I smiled, turning to face Sandy.

"I need to go to the toilet." She moaned in pain trying to pull herself up from the chair. I helped Sandy to her feet and walked her to the toilets, she was on a walking frame so I didn't have to do much. Just make sure she is steady and doesn't fall.

I love working on this ward because the ladies were normally so kind and always up for a chat. They loved it even more when Neil would come in and hand out the lunches, he got harassed daily but he loved the attention.

Once Sandy was sorted and back on her bed, I went over to Tracy who is 76 and currently recovering from a knee replacement as well. She has terrible Parkinson's, which affects her voice. In the morning you'll be able to hear her but when the hours ticked on her voice becomes more delicate. She reminded me of my nan with her thin wrinkly skin and grey thin hair.

"I need to wee," she whispered.

"Tracy, you have a catheter in, so you won't need to go to the toilet!" I shouted trying to get her to understand me.

I turned my back to walk out the door and heard a crash on the floor, I looked straight over to Tracy who was covered in water. My eyes travelled down to her cup on the floor.

"Oh, Tracy," I said walking over to her.

"Sorry, my dear," she said, trying to clean herself up.

"No, no," I ordered at her.

"Don't move, I'll clean it up." I smiled at her. I mopped up the water and helped change Tracy into a clean gown for the fifth time today. I filled up the glass halfway and gave it to her. Her thin fingers wrapped around the glass and lifted the glass to her mouth. Once she was done, I placed the cup on the bedside table and moved it away from her.

It soon turned 7 o'clock and that was my queue to leave.

I said my goodbyes and hastily left. I walked through the long corridors, made my way past the sharp bends and got into my car. The clouds were grey and the air was still. A thunderstorm was afoot and I couldn't be more excited.

Something about storms soothes me, it's strangely comforting watching the sky lose control for a while. The boom of the thunder started whilst I was driving home. I was aching to see a flash of purple bright light.

Once I got home, Rover was waiting for me on the bed.

"Hello buddy," I said, flopping myself on the bed next to him, giving him a big cuddle, leaning my head on his fluffy belly.

I heard a rumble come from his belly that wasn't the blasting thunderstorm outside.

"Okay, dinner time then," I laughed.

A crackle bled through the sky lighting the kitchen with a bright spark.

"Here you go piglet." I placed Rover's dinner down giving him less than 15 seconds to finish it all.

Later that night after dinner, Rover and I sat down on my bed and cuddled up and slowly fell asleep. All I could hear was the angry rain and the wild winds outside…I was in my own slice of heaven.

***

"Tell me why we are going to the gym at six in the morning on our day off," Iris huffed slamming the door of my truck.

"Because it's a good way to start the day and I'm fed up with hearing my mum tell me I've put on weight," I said, forcing a smile on my face.

What I really wanted to tell her was that Mark was on my mind and has been for the last couple of days. I couldn't help but fall asleep thinking about him and what he's doing. I've tried so hard for the past six months to forget him and I have, mostly…Plus my jeans no longer button up so the gym it is.

"I feel like I look like Legolas today," I said trying to sort my hair out in the gym mirror.

"Who?" Iris screwed her face up, taking off the 10 kg weights of the bar.

"The elf from Lord of the rings," I answered taking the 16kg off the bar.

"What?" she said with her face still screwed up in a tight ball.

"With the bow and arrow…" I moved my arms and did a shooting arrow motion, putting the weights on the floor.

"Oh, never mind," I said, turning back to the mirror.

This is how it's gonna be, huh? Not gonna work with me today? I said to myself trying to sort out the bumps in my hair.

"Screw it," I huffed.

"Do you need help lifting those?" I heard a voice beside me and there stood the two men that I hated most in this world. I didn't know their names but I saw them every time I came to the gym. They must be in their early 60s, I could tell by the greying hair and wrinkled tattoos that travelled up their arms. They prayed on weak girls in the gym, luckily for me I was not one of them so they rarely spoke to me but I've seen the way they look and talk to girls.

"Nope, I'm good thanks." I smiled, lifting the weights and plopping them down by my seat ready for a set.

As I looked up they were both laughing, all I wanted to do at that point was drop the weights on their stupid old faces but, sometimes you've got to rise above other people's behaviours.

We finished our last set on the shoulder press and moved on to the chest press machine and I noticed as I was drinking some water the two men followed us to the chest press and I can see in the mirror one was staring at my bum.

You know I said sometimes you've got to rise above? Yeah, well, screw that.

"Can you not?" I turned around immediately catching both of them laughing.

"Excuse me, doll?" one smirked.

"Stop staring at me, I can see you in the mirror. I see the way you look at women and I've had enough of it. If you want to stare, do it somewhere else, don't come near me," I snapped and put my headphones back on my head.

"Well go on!" I shouted as they just stood there flabbergasted.

I'm not sure what gave men the right to be able to treat women the way they do. Especially at the gym, I see it all the time. Just because you are a male does not mean I need help with everything because I am seen as the weaker sex.

***

Alice and Thomas asked me to babysit tonight and I jumped at the chance. I'd do anything to spend time with my niece Libby and new nephew Henry.

Alice gave birth to Henry two days after I returned from Portugal.

He weighed 7lbs, born at two in the afternoon and he was beautiful. Dark-haired, brown-eyed angel.

I pulled into their driveway and I could hear the screaming from my car.

"Libby Valerie Miller you do not do that to your brother!" I heard Alice shout.

Uh-oh.

"Your saviour has arrived," I said, knocking on the front door.

"Welcome to the madhouse," Thomas said, letting me in.

"That sounded intense," I laughed.

"Libby has put Sudocrem all over Henry," he said with a deflating breath.

I could see the newborn was taking a toll on him. The dark circles under his eyes gave him away, plus the new wrinkles and weight loss.

"Alice!" I shouted up the stairs.

"Just leave it and I'll sort it all out," I continued hearing an exhausted huff escape her mouth followed by her heavy tired footsteps coming down the stairs.

"Did I ever tell you I loved you?" she smiled and handed me over a Henry covered in Sudocrem, which was now in my hair.

"Not nearly enough," I muttered.

"What was that?" she said.

"Nothing, now leave." I shooed them out the door.

Right, think Bellamy first things first get Henry in the bath.

"Can I join?" I heard Libby come into the bathroom.

"If only you promise not to do this to your brother again," I said looking at her.

I found it hard to tell her off, her lovely long blonde hair in a loose ponytail, her big blue eyes beaming. She was so freaking adorable.

I finished running the bath and put Henry in his seat, where he then started to splash and kick, making the water go everywhere.

"Okay, you crazy boy," I laughed patting the water from my face, trying to get the cream out of his hair.

"Libby, comes on darling," I called. I washed Libby's hair and stopped another war when Henry nearly kicked Libby in the face.

I felt so happy being here with them. I cannot wait to be a mum and I know it's never normally like this because I've babysat for them, William and Sarah, enough to know kids are hard work. I lifted Libby out of the bath and wrapped her in a towel and then I picked Henry up and did the same.

Placing Henry on the bed, I clothed him, gave him his bottle and very shortly he was asleep in my arms. I motioned to Libby to be quiet as I carried Henry to bed. I turned on the night light and silently closed the door.

"Please, can you plait my hair?" Libby asked, still wrapped in her towel like a burrito.

"Of course angel, but first let's get you dressed." I guided Libby's left and right foot into the appropriate holes followed by her arms and head.

"Perfect." I smiled as I then tried to tackle her hair.

It took me half an hour to do her hair. Half a bloody hour.

"Are you done yet?" Libby yawned.

"Nearly," I said, struggling to get her long hair tied away.

Probably should have told her I can't plait hair.

Chapter Thirteen
Bellamy

Mum invited me over for lunch today and I was really looking forward to it. I had today off at the hospital and I won't be back at the pub till three and I missed her.

I started working at the pub a couple of weeks after I came back from Portugal and I liked working at the pub, it gave me a little bit of pocket money to put back into my savings. The people that I worked with were very nice, which made it so much easier because I was extremely nervous and it took me all day to learn how to pour a pint, it's not as easy as it looks, believes me.

"I forgot to mention I have hired a gardener. Your dad and I are just getting too old now." Mum spoke, coming over to block my view from the TV.

"Good for you," I replied looking up at her.

"Here we go," Dad said, lifting himself up from his chair and retreating into the kitchen.

Suspicious.

"Well, I thought maybe he could come over for lunch one day," she said innocently.

"Yeah, that would be nice for you," I replied, she was acting weird…why?

"Well, yes, I thought so too so he's coming over for lunch," she said with a cheeky grin across her face.

"So you mentioned," I said trying to figure out where she was going with this.

"In about ten minutes," Mum blurted out before walking back into the kitchen.

"Wait what? Oh, Jesus Christ, Mum really?" I pinched my eyebrows feeling a headache coming on.

I knew what she was doing and I didn't know what was worse, my mum trying to set me up out of kindness or getting to the point where I needed her help.

Dad appeared from the kitchen with a glass full of brown liquid.

"Thanks," I said, taking the glass.

I was sipping my whiskey nervously shaking my leg when I heard the door ring and that sip turned into a gulp. "I'll get it," Mum ran towards the door. Maybe I could run outside and play with the dog for a couple of hours?

Maybe that would look a little bit weird...

"Come in, I'd like you to meet my daughter and husband." I heard Mum walking into the lounge. Shit. Shit. Shit.

"This is—" Mum started to say until I looked up and locked eyes with him.

"Holy shit," I felt the colour drain from my face.

"Bellamy," and there stood in front of me the man I've been trying to forget for the past six months.

"You two know each other?" Dad asked.

"This just got so much better," Dad continued with a grin from ear to ear.

He looked so different yet so familiar. His hair was slightly longer and his beard had grown. My eyes rolled from

145

his face down his red tartan shirt, past his black jeans and ended at his walking boots. He looked bigger, muscular and somehow taller. His eyes still shone a beautiful blue.

"Does someone care to explain?" my mum asked, her eyes looking back and forth at us both.

"We met in Portugal," Mark replied, not taking his eyes off me.

I was completely speechless. I just downed the rest of my whiskey letting the liquid burn my throat.

"Would you care for a drink?" I asked.

"No? Okay, just me then," I said before letting anyone else get a word in.

"Excuse me." I moved between Mark and Mum and went straight into the kitchen, pouring myself another whiskey, a large whiskey.

"Need some help?" he looked at me already downing my second.

"Okay, maybe you do need my help you won't be able to stand soon," Mark laughed.

"What are you doing here?" I asked.

"I did say I was staying around London for a while."

"You said you were staying in London, not bloody Essex, which isn't exactly in London," I said frustrated.

"Admit it, you're glad to see me." A smirk crossed his face.

"Oh, Jesus bloody Christ," were the only words I was able to muster.

Mark:

She looked as amazing as ever but that didn't surprise me.

Her hair was blonder, her freckles were no longer taking over her face. She looked good, healthy and damn this woman made me nervous.

Watching her go to pour her third glass of whiskey I took the bottle out of her hand.

"I don't think that's necessary," I said.

"Oh, trust me it's necessary," she said trying to grab the bottle out of my hand.

"Not gonna happen, sweetheart," I said, lifting the bottle high up towards the ceiling.

"Give me the whiskey," she demanded.

"No."

"Mark."

"Bellamy."

"Don't make me kick you in the balls." She raised her eyebrows.

"You're very aggressive."

"And you're insufferable," she said, lifting herself up on her tiptoes, trying to reach the bottle. She was so close to me, I could smell the coconut on her skin.

"You look like an annoyed little guinea pig," I laughed.

I shouldn't be winding her up further but I couldn't help myself.

"You're a dick!" she spat.

"Charming as ever," I replied.

"Am I interrupting something?" I heard Bellamy's mum say from the open archway. Not realising we were standing toe to toe with Bellamy still trying to reach for the bottle.

"No." I heard Bellamy say whilst clearing her throat, leaning back on the balls of her feet.

"Your poor dog has been standing by the door for five minutes so please go get him in and wipe his paws down, the last thing I need is muddy paw prints on my carpet."

I almost laughed watching this grown woman getting ordered around by her mum.

Within five minutes, I was back in the lounge watching a massive pile of fluff run over to me. "Rover, don't jump." I heard Bellamy call out.

"Hello, boy," I said, giving him a cuddle.

Rover replied by licking my face.

"Oh, thank you," I said.

"He likes you," I heard Bellamy's father from his chair.

"That makes one of us," Bellamy muttered. What was up this girl's arse today?

"It's very nice to meet you, sir. Apologies for not introducing myself sooner, seeing your daughter again kind of put my mind on a spin," I said, shaking her father's hand.

"No worries mate, you want a beer?" he asked.

I liked him already.

"No thank you, I've got to see my aunt later," I said, although that beer did sound bloody lovely.

"I'll just finish up lunch, please everyone, sit at the table." Beth Bellamy's mum said with a massive smile planted across her face but the only thing I heard was what sounded like a growl coming out of Bellamy's mouth.

Beth laid out an amazing buffet styled afternoon tea and it all looked amazing.

I felt something nudging at my elbow, looking down to see Rover and his big brown eyes just begging for food.

"Rover, bed," Bellamy said sharply looking over at him with raised eyebrows. He didn't move a muscle.

"Rover!" she raised her voice, after that he walked back to his bed with his head low and huffed as he planted himself down.

"That was amazing," I said after finishing my last bite. "Thank you." I smiled and looked over at Bellamy who didn't say a word through lunch or even looked at me.

"I'll clear up," Bellamy said, raising herself from her chair and neatly piling the plates on top of each other.

After the table was cleared, Bellamy walked back in with a whiskey.

Silly girl.

"Where are you staying?" Paul Bellamy's father said.

He was a very nice man and extremely easy to talk to.

"I'm currently staying at my auntie's, on top of her pub for now, until I get my clientele back up and then I'll buy some place, hopefully."

"What pub?" Bellamy asked.

"The baked goose," I replied and within that moment Bellamy let out a grunt and face planted the table.

"Jesus Christ," was all I could hear her say.

"Oh bell, isn't that the pub you work at?" Beth looked as surprised as I felt.

"Yes," she said, muffled by the table cloth.

Now I understand.

Maeve is my aunt, who is Bellamy's boss and now I'm staying at the top of that pub.

How fantastic!

Things were really looking good for me, I couldn't help but smile.

Later that day – Bellamy:

"A beer please, my lady."

149

"Sure, coming right up," I replied to Phil.

Phil was a 70-year-old divorced man and always gave good tips on a Friday.

"Now that's what I like to see whilst I pour a pint," Anne said interrupting my thoughts.

I looked over to see she was talking about Mark.

There were two big doors and windows leading out to the garden and he was mowing the lawn. "Yes, a shame he's gay," I said.

"What!" Anna shouted.

"Yep, big old gay," I said looking over at the extremely beautiful man just doing the most simplistic of a task.

I didn't mean to be so rude to him at mums, but I thought it would be easier if I didn't like him.

I don't want to spend time with him because he would leave again and then I'd have to go through this whole thing again and I simply can't do that to myself.

"Oh, bloody hell, you're joking," Anna laughed, shaking her head. "They're either gay or taken these days," she then finished.

"Tell me about it." I smiled, handing Phil his beer.

Phil looked at me knowing full well Mark was not gay. I just raised my eyebrows and shrugged my shoulders.

I was working till close so I decided to take an early break.

I sat on the back doorstep drinking my water when a sudden breeze came rushing towards me. February was coming and I loved the colder weather.

Big baggy jumpers, snuggling up with Rover on the sofa watching The Lord of the Rings. Heaven.

Six hours later, I rang the last order bell and I couldn't have been more pleased. A waitress called in sick so we were extremely understaffed. I took the last payment from a table and locked the door. This was the busiest shift I have done since I started working here.

"So." I heard a very familiar voice behind me.

"Jesus Christ," I said, jumping out of my skin.

"I have a question," Mark said, crossing his arms and leaning against the kitchen door.

"Well go on then," I said cleaning up the last table.

"Have you been telling people I'm gay?"

I froze.

"Nope," I said, shrugging my shoulders and carrying on with picking up the plates.

"Are you sure?" Mark stalked across the room towards me.

"I'm pretty certain." I smiled.

As he walked towards me, I walked backwards trying to keep the distance.

"I don't believe you." He frowned.

"That's not my problem," I said before realising the distance between us was gone and my back was against the locked door.

"I've missed you," he said, his eyes searching my face like it was a treasure in the palm of his hands.

"I thought you'd be happy?" he said.

"Well, I'm not," I lied, Mark's face screwed up into a ball. "Why?"

"Did you ever think of me?" I couldn't help but ask, ignoring his question.

He was standing so close to me, I could smell his aftershave and it was intoxicating.

"Every single day, Bellamy. Every single long, horrible day. How could you ever leave my mind? I kept thinking that another man noticed how beautiful you are and wanted to make you his. I'd fall asleep wondering what you are doing, who you're with."

He took a step back and he looked miserable and frustrated.

"Why didn't you text me, you could have called, we could have tried?" he urged.

"Because I didn't want to have to forget you. Again. If I did text you, then I'd just be holding on to someone I couldn't have."

"You can have me now," he said with his full and bright eyes looking into mine.

"But will you stay?" I said feeling powerless.

Please stay.

Please want me.

"I never wanted to leave in the first place."

A small smile crossed my face and I didn't know what else to do but hug him. Inhaling his scent and feeling his muscles under my palms.

"Let's do something tomorrow," Mark suggested, pulling away from our hug and placing a kiss on my forehead.

I was not going to settle for a kiss on the forehead, not after all this time.

"That's not how you kiss a girl, Mr Barnes," I smirked.

My hands cupped his cheeks, I studied his face, just wanting to take in the sight of him the sight that I've longed to see, the lips I've wanted to kiss, the lips I have seen in my dreams.

Nervousness and excitement filled my stomach.

I leaned up on my tiptoes, my head turned left whilst he turned right and I softly kissed him. I felt the warmth of his body pressed up against me and the taste of his breath lingered on my mouth.

I let my lips linger, extremely close to his but not yet touching.

My arms wrapped around his neck whilst his hands travelled up my body slowly, feeling every curve and bump, then they stopped on my face. His thumb made slow circles on my cheek and his lips plunged into mine, allowing our tongues to tie. This kiss went from slow to heavy rather quickly.

"Wow," Mark said, breathing heavily.

"That's my line," I laughed while kissing him one more time.

"I'll see you tomorrow, Barnes," I said, grabbing my bag and leaving through the back way towards my truck.

The Next day – Bellamy:

I drove to the pub with Rover in the back seat.

It was the time of year when dogs were allowed on the beach and he loved the sand.

Mine and Mark's kiss still lingered in my mind.

I could still taste him on my swollen lips when I got home.

A loud woof escaped Rover's mouth.

"Listen, Mark is coming so that's why you are sitting in the back so don't start with me," I said looking back at Rover sulking.

Mark walked out of the pub in black jeans, a white hoodie and a denim jacket with fleece lining.

"Damn," I whispered to myself as I watched him place his hands in his jacket pockets.

"Nice car." Mark smiled as he got into my truck.

"Thank you."

"Hi, Rover boy." Mark leaned over to the back seat and gave Rover a stroke.

I started to drive and I turned on my randoms playlist on my Spotify.

"Oh, I love this song." I turned the volume up to, *wasn't me* by shaggy.

"You let her catch you?" I mimicked.

"I don't know how I let this happen," I continued.

"With who?" Mark interrupted.

"The girl next door, you know," I replied.

"Man." He shook his head.

"I don't know what to do."

"Say it wasn't you," he mocked.

"Alright." I nodded.

We both burst out laughing as we sung in the car like fools. For a moment I felt as if we were both back in Portugal laughing by the side of the pool, relaxing in the sun. Enjoying our company just like we are now. It's been a while since I had laughed like this, especially with a man. To have a friendship, a level of comfort to sing along in a car with a man feels all too rare.

I parked at the beach, and started our walked along the sandy rock.

"Okay question time," I said looking over at him.

"How old were you when you had your first kiss?" I asked.

"Ten."

I raised my eyebrow, ten…

"You?" Mark asked shoving my shoulder.

"17." I blushed

"Prude." He replied slightly

We both laughed. Again. My cheeks were starting to hurt.

"Okay, my turn." Mark turned to me.

"Which pill would you take...Red pill? You'll get to restart your life at the age of ten with all the knowledge you have now or blue pill? You jump to being 50 years old with 50 million pounds?"

I took a deep breath, looked over at Rover and then back at Mark.

"Red pill. I took so much for granted when I was younger, I suppose we all do. I'd go to school and actually listen. I'd learn. I'd defiantly tell more people to fuck off. I would have spent more time with people that I knew didn't have long left. However, saying this, if I didn't go through what I went through I wouldn't be the person I am today."

"Interesting...I take it you was a little shit at school," he laughed.

"Such a little shit," I laughed back.

I noticed Rover started pulling on the lead.

"Rover stop!" I yelled tugging at his lead as I planted my feet in the ground.

"Do you need some help?" Mark asked.

"I'm good," I said until Rover saw a pigeon. "No, Rover, don't do it!" I warned him and then just like a naughty child he took one look at me and ran into the water, pulling me with him.

"Rover!" I screamed as my knees buckled and my head went under the water.

Scrambling up on my feet I noticed whilst I nearly drowned Rover came out of the water and was sitting next to Mark.

"I'm gonna kill you," I said pointing towards the dog.

"And you." I then pointed at Mark who was too busy laughing.

"I didn't do anything?" he said.

"That's the point," I said.

"Shit, it's really cold," I said as the water was dripping off my hair onto my arms.

"Come here," Mark said taking off his denim jacket, placing it over my shoulders.

"Thank you." I shivered.

"I'm not talking to you," I spat at Rover who was walking nicely next to me.

We quickly got back in my truck and I turned the heating on full blast.

"Fucking hell," I said still shivering.

"Are you alright?" he asked, placing a hand on my thigh.

I looked over at him with a frown.

Am I okay?

No, I'm soaking wet, and I'm pretty sure I'm gonna catch hypothermia.

"Taking that as a no," Mark said slowly lifting his hand off my thigh.

Mark:

Once we got back to Bellamy's flat, she ran straight into her bedroom, grabbed some clothes and then announced she was going to have a shower and won't be long.

20 minutes later, Bellamy appeared from the bathroom with leggings on, a jumper and her hair up in a messy bun.

"Sexy right?" she smiled, turning around.

"Extremely," I chuckled.

If she only knew how sexy she looked to me.

I watched her laugh to herself and move towards the sofa.

I'm looking at her right now and goodness gracious me, she is the one.

"That was a very interesting date," she said pulling me out of my daydream.

"Shall we order a pizza and watch a movie?" she asked grabbing her Mac off the coffee table and placing it on her lap.

"Are you coming?" she asked and looked down at the space next to her.

"Yeah, sure." I smiled, rubbing the back of my neck.

Why do I feel this way? My stomach was turning, my heart was racing…

"Mr Barnes, are you nervous?" she asked.

"Pfft no." I shrugged.

"You are!" she gasped. "Oh my God!" she laughed out loud clapping her hands together.

I walked over to the sofa and sat next to Bellamy.

"Shut up." I nudged her.

"What do you want to watch?" I asked.

"Lord of the rings?" she smiled.

I looked over at her disapprovingly.

"Taking that as a no," she whispered.

"Fine, you choose and I'll order pizza." She began tapping away on her mac book.

I flicked through the movies on Netflix and saw Harry Potter, I shrugged and put it on. Let's give this a go.

"Didn't pin you for the Harry Potter type," she said looking at me.

"I've never seen it," I admitted.

"Mr Barnes!" she gasped.

"I'm so excited for you!" she shrieked with excitement.

Two hours later, Bellamy had fallen asleep on my shoulder with Rover curled up behind her legs, leaning his head on her bum.

The empty pizza box sat there and I couldn't help myself. I moved very slowly and got up, leaving Bellamy's head on a cushion.

I picked up the box and the glasses, walked over to the sink and Rover followed me and sat by the back door.

"Yes, sir," I said unlocking the back down to let him out.

"I'm sorry did I fall asleep?" I heard a sleepy voice behind me.

I turned around to see Bellamy rubbing her sleepy eyes.

"You did indeed." I smiled walking over to her, cupping her face and lightly kissing her. "I need to make a move," I announced as a groan escaped her mouth. I leaned back into her lips silencing her before she could talk.

"Okay, I really need to go," I said, leaning away. "You keep your distance," I said pointing at her.

"Ugh God," I groaned, running back to her, "I can't seem to help myself more, stay away." My lips smashed against hers whilst she laughed, "Okay bye," I said walking out the door.

Chapter Fourteen
Bellamy

"You can't pull your cannula out darling, you need this okay?"

I spoke softly to Ada trying to reassure her. I patted her hand and went to walk away but then her hand reached out for mine, I sat down beside her bed which isn't meant to sound as creepy as it does. Ada had such heard 78. No one comes to visit her anymore. Her husband used to, but he became ill long ago, she rarely recognised him but his smile never faded and neither did his love for her.

"You look like my child I lost years ago. Her name was Mary." She took a deep breath, shaking her head in disbelief.

"No mother should lose their child. It's a fate worse than death." Her weak, fragile hand cupped my cheek.

"You dear, look just like her, I can't quite believe it." My eyes welled up looking at her soft wrinkled face looking at me with such love and sorrow.

"Don't cry, a face like yours should never feel sadness." If only she knew for a while of my life that's all I felt.

"Thank you, Ada." I squeezed her hand.

"Truly," I whispered as I got up and walked out of the ward and straight to the toilets.

I ran the cold water over my face. It took me a while to compose myself that was heavy and not what I was expecting today and nether was this reaction.

"Bellamy, they need you downstairs!" Taya shouted, knocking on the toilet door.

"Yep coming," I replied, waving my hands in front of my face, trying to cool my red skin.

After my rounds of taking temperatures and blood pressure for preoperative assessments, I made my way back upstairs to see chaos in the halls.

"What's happened?" I asked a nurse who looked rather flushed.

"A lady has passed away," she said walking away.

My stomach dropped and in my heart, I knew it was Ada.

I walked into her room my mouth running dry and there she was.

"She just closed her eyes and fell asleep." Taya came up behind me wiping her eyes.

"I know they said don't get attached but that woman was something else," Taya continued with a smile.

"I need to go." I turned and made my way through the hospital, a sigh of relief escaped my mouth when I saw the large doors leading outside.

I felt sick to my stomach, my chest felt tight, my feet became unsteady as my hands began to tremble.

I tried to take in a deep breath to calm myself but my breaths were sharp and shallow.

I stumbled to my car, sat down as I tried to let it pass.

It took an hour but my breath finally slowed, my sweats stopped, my heart slowed down and I was able to drive home.

The first thing I did was check my mail and there it was, the letter from the company that I applied to for the paramedic apprenticeship. I anxiously opened the letter and read.

We regret to inform you but you were not successful, I only needed to read those word to know what the rest of the letter said.

My heart sank.

For the second time today.

I folded the letter and pressed it against my chest, took a deep breath and chuckled. How silly I was to think they'd offer me a space. What a fool.

I called Mum and she agreed to let Rover stay there so I had the flat to myself. I didn't let my mum ask questions as I quickly dropped the dog off and returned to my truck. Once I got home I got dressed into my pyjamas and dragged myself to the sofa where my legs gave way.

I never turned the TV on. I never moved.

It wasn't until I opened my eyes again that I felt it.

The dark cloud of depression almost swallowed me whole within a second. It consumed me quickly. As if someone had turned on a switch in my head.

Everything went quiet and the voice slowly reappeared in my head like a lion hunting its prey.

I was soon aching for nightfall and the darkness to close my eyes and not wake up.

I want to sleep because when I sleep it goes away, a little moment of peace but the voice was so loud, terrorising my brain, destroying any source of happiness and peace.

Depression isn't beautiful, poetic or fashionable, it's darkness, it's loneliness, numbing, deafening and horribly addictive.

Mark:

I turned up at Bellamy's parents as they wanted me over every week to spend an hour in their garden mowing the lawn and tending to the weeds, which I was more than happy to do.

My clientele was slowly growing every week and soon I was fully booked, I may have to look at more staff soon, this one-man band was taking on a lot of work.

I normally let myself in at the back gate and carry all my equipment through. I unlocked the gate, and was surprised to see an energetic Rover running up to me.

"Hey, puppy." I smiled coming to his level, squishing his face between my hands.

"Where's your mum, I haven't heard from her in a couple of days." Rover just looked up at me wagging his tail.

I've texted Bellamy a couple of times and she hasn't spoken to me in three days, which concerned me, but I knew she worked long, unsociable hours at the hospital. Therefore, I just thought maybe she's exhausted and I knew she would text me when she was ready.

Half an hour into the job, Bellamy's mum Beth came into the garden and called Rover into the house.

"Hello, Mark." Beth called.

"Good morning." I smiled.

"Would you mind if I had a word with you?" she asked.

"Of course," I said, walking over to her.

Beth led me back into the lounge and sat down on the sofa.

I went to take my boots off and enter the house.

"Oh, please don't worry," she fussed.

"Is everything okay?" I asked, now starting to worry.

"Two years ago, Bellamy tried to take her own life." Oh my God.

"I found her in the bath, she had taken sleeping pills, and a mixture of other things."

I felt sick.

"She hasn't shown up for work or even picked Rover up after like she normally does." Beth started to tear up and my heart broke for her.

The pure worry of a mother.

"I've tried, Iris has tried, but she won't open the door. She has read all the messages we have sent, and we know she wants to be alone." She pulled out a key from her pocket.

"This is her spare key. I had one made when she got the flat." I took it and held it in the palm of my hands.

"Please go and see her. I'm hoping you might be able to talk to her. I know it's a lot to ask but she's changed ever since you got here, the last person she will want to see is any of us," she said with a tear rolling down her cheek.

"Beth, I love your daughter," I said, placing my hand on hers.

I love her.

I love her.

Of course, I love her I loved her since the day I met her.

"If you don't mind, I'm going to go now." I lifted myself up from the sofa, feeling an ache and panic in my chest that I'd never felt before.

"Thank you, Mark," I heard her say as I closed the front door.

I don't know what to say to Bellamy. I don't know how to comfort her but I knew I'd be damned if I let anything happen to her whilst I'm alive and breathing. I got straight in the van, cancelled everything for the next two days and I drove to her apartment.

I put the key in the lock and opened the door to see nothing but darkness, no lights and the blinds were all pulled.

My eyes wandered over the apartment until they stopped on a figure leaning against a wall. It was Bellamy, she was hugging her knees to her chest and her head was tucked in.

She looked like a frightened, fragile child.

"Bellamy," I whispered. No answer.

I closed the door, walked towards the dark shape on the floor and bent down to meet her.

"Bellamy, are you okay?" I asked feeling helpless.

The beautiful, confident, fierce woman I fell in love with was not there. I wasn't getting a response so I decided to take matters into my own hands. I scooped her up in my arms and walked her over to the sofa. I bent in front of her, unfolding her arms and moved the stray hairs from her face.

"I've been so worried about you," I said, her head finally, slowly raised as her eyes met mine.

"I'm scaring myself, Mark," she whispered, those words dug into my heart like nails.

"How long has it been?" she asked.

"Three days." I didn't know what else to say, so I held her in my arms.

After an hour, she started to relax and I knew she was going to be okay because I was here now. I walked around the apartment and lifted the blinds. The late morning light lit up the apartment. Once I sat back down on the couch, she hugged me, wrapped her arms around my neck and my arms naturally pulled her close. "Thank you," she whispered into my neck.

Bellamy:

Being wrapped in Mark's arms made me feel safe.

I pulled away and stood up from the sofa, I instantly got light-headed, I leant back gripping the sofa for support.

"Are you okay?" Mark asked instantly coming to my aid.

"Yeah," I replied grabbing my stomach.

"When was the last time you ate?" he asked.

I looked him in the eyes and simply replied. "Three days ago."

His face dropped.

"I'll be right back," he said, kissing my forehand. He walked towards the kitchen. I could hear him looking through the cupboards and then he walked into the bathroom and started running the bath.

Five minutes later he kneeled down in front of me again. "I've run you a bath," he said, I took his large hand in mine and let him lead me to the bathroom.

"Please take a bath and I'll be back in ten minutes okay?" he asked. I nodded and watched him walk out, leaving the door open.

I undressed myself and stood naked in my bathroom I made a huge mistake when I decided to look at myself in the mirror.

There was no life left in my face.

I wanted to be strong, I wanted to get through this, but a part of me, the voice, didn't want me to be strong anymore.

I just want to be at peace.

I sat down in the warm bath and washed my body and hair.

I can do this.
I can do this.

I repeated to myself over and over again. After a while I lifted myself from the water and wrapped my dressing gown tightly across my body.

I walked out the open door and saw Mark cooking eggs and bacon.

He turned around and smiled at me, taking my breath away. He took two plates out of the cupboard and served the food.

"Here," he said as he placed one plate on one side and one in front of him.

He was eating with me and I knew why.

They did this in the psych ward with patients who suffered from eating disorders, some felt comfort when eating with another.

I looked down at the food and I felt sick to my stomach. "You can do this," Mark reassured me.

I cut the egg, looked at it, took a deep breath and placed it in my mouth. A smile crept across my face, "This is good."

The corners of his mouth turned up, looking extremely pleased with himself.

"I was thinking after this we could watch a movie?" he asked finishing up his eggs and bacon never looking away from me.

"I'd like that." I smiled weakly

An hour later, I put on clean light pink PJs and joined Mark on the sofa.

"Lord of the rings?" He asked, a grin grew on my face with excitement.

"I thought you'd like it." He beamed.

"May I?" he asked coming to sit next to me.

"Please," I begged.

He sat down beside me and pulled me in close and he never let go.

Throughout the whole film, he never let me go.

As the credits rolled, I felt the black cloud over my head lift. It was as simple as that.

As quickly as it came, it left.

I took a deep breath feeling free again.

"Are you okay?" Mark said moving so he could see me better.

"At this moment in time, I hold so much shame for my body. As if I am less lovable because of my weight. I cut the labels out of my clothes so I don't have to see the size because I define my worth on a number."

I took a deep breath and carried on, letting the words full out of my mouth.

"I do not wish to live in a world where I feel less worthy of love or attention because of how my body looks. There was a moment yesterday when I thought I could give up now, I can let go and I won't have to fight anymore."

I let my head fall into my hands, squeezing my eyes shut trying to keep in the tears that were threatening to escape my eyes.

"Oh Bell," Mark whispered. "I love you." He let out a sigh of relief lifting my chin.

"Do you understand I love you and I do not want to live in a world where a Bellamy Edmondson does not exist?"

"How can you love me when I cannot love myself? I do not understand, I'm so broken Mark, I have these stretch marks all over my body. I'm horrible, the voices—" He grabbed my face, not letting me finish the sentence.

"I don't know if I can make this any clearer, but I love you, all of you. I don't care," he said rising to his feet.

"I don't care if you have stretch marks. I don't care about any of those superficial things, the only thing I care about is loving you."

He then knelt in front of me and pressed both hands on my cheeks.

"No stretch mark is gonna stop me wanting you. When I'm loving you, I'm loving all of you."

"Wait…" I stopped him, his hands leaving my cheeks.

"You really love me?" I looked straight into his eyes.

"Madly," he replied, placing a light kiss on my cheek.

This guy, this man loved me. Me? Bellamy Edmondson.

My hands came down to his which where resting on my thighs, I gripped them tight, "You have no idea how much I love you too…" I confessed.

"Madly." I laughed as he placed a kiss on my lips. Words could no longer express our feelings.

I have fallen in love with him. Fully and completely in love with him and that scares me more than anything. He has my heart, he's capable of destroying me, he could shatter me into a million pieces and the worst thing is I would let him. Because I love him, I love him in a way that consumes me.

"I want you, in every way possible." I stood up and walked towards my room, I stopped and turned around once I came to the open doorway. I fiddled with the ends of my clothes, as his eyes never left my body.

"Are you sure?" he asked, I nodded, my body now burning with desire and a need for him to touch me.

Slowly, he slipped his shoes off and pulled his top off over his head. Revelling a brawny, well-defined chest, I had craved this body for 6 months and here it was so close and all mine.

"You are my always," Mark said.

"Do you understand? I am here for the long run. This is not just a pit stop for me." His face changed into a look of hunger and need.

"Mark Barnes, just shut up and get yourself over here." I demined.

We made love twice that night and he left me trembling three times under his touch.

I came to understand what it felt like to not have to fake it, which also seems a rarity nowadays.

I may not have had much experience with men but with him, everything came naturally. *Excuse the pun*. When a man is fully imbedding himself inside you, there is no other feeling quite like it.

Mark:

Waking up to Bellamy curled up in my arms felt fucking marvellous.

"How are you feeling?" I asked her.

She stretched leaning into my chest and turned around to face me.

"Achy," she groaned but with a smile that told me, I could do it again anytime, which I very much plan on doing.

"I'm still getting over my past but I have to say, you have helped me move on. I'm extremely grateful for what we have, whatever it is we have. I'm so grateful for you," she suddenly confessed as her hand came up to my cheek, her thumb moving in slow, circular movements.

"I love you," I said, I wanted to say it and remind her every second of everyday that I loved her.

"Madly." She beamed.

"I don't deserve you," she whispered.

"No, you deserved more," I replied.

Bellamy kissed me, sat up, swung her leg over me and relaxed into my lap, I leaned up to meet her, a moan escaping my mouth as I kissed her.

"Are you hungry?" she asked in between kisses.

"For you? Yes," I mocked, kissing her neck.

She lifted herself off my lap, pushing herself away from me.

"No, no, no!" I moaned trying to grab her and place her back where she belonged.

"I'm going to make breakfast," she laughed and slapped my hands away.

She jumped off the bed... but before she reached the open door her face met the floor with a hard.

thump

"I'm okay, I'm okay," Bellamy said getting up from off the floor, "I've got to stop doing that," she huffed and exited the room.

Chapter Fifteen
A Couple of Weeks Later – Bellamy

When I asked Mark to come to my brother's birthday gathering, I didn't actually expect him to say yes. Meeting someone's family is a big thing, right? Well…when I say I asked Mark, we were over at Mum's for the afternoon and she mentioned the party and invited him. I'm so grateful for her big mouth sometimes.

I had just finished my hair when I heard a knock on the door.

"Coming!" I called as I made my way and unlocked the door.

He wore black jeans, a black shirt with small white prints and a leather jacket.

"Really?" I asked still looking at him.

"What?" he laughed looking down at his outfit.

"How do you do it, Mr Barnes?" I asked but before he could answer.

"Hold that thought," I put my index finger in the air before walking to the back door, letting Rover out, closing the back door and made my way to the man of my dreams. I started by taking off his jacket, he raised an eyebrow as he watched my every move, I cupped his face, taking a moment to look at him and I see the man I love, the man that makes everything make sense. I kissed him aching for his lips on mine, his arms in response wrapped around my waist.

I slowly pulled his buttons undone on his shirt one by one.

"What are you doing?" he asked.

"Just shut up," I replied, attacking his lips with mine.

Mark's arms reached down my thighs and lifted me up I giggled into his mouth as a low chuckle escaped his.

Happiness doesn't even begin to cover it.

"Where going to be late for your brother's birthday," Mark said in between kisses.

"Not important," I said, kissing him back.

We both fell on the floor with Mark on top of me. His hands went down to my trousers, undone the buttons, then stopped, he leaned up and pulled his shirt off. My hands reached up and undid his belt. I leaned up to meet him as I pulled my top over my head.

"You've never taken your top off in front of me before." Mark he stopped his eyes burning while in my chest.

"I mean… we can sit down and talk about it or you can do something about it." I raised my eyebrows and with that our clothes came off and Mark made me scream, twice.

Mark:

After 40 minutes we laid on the floor tangled up in each other's arms, I was completely naked and Bellamy just had her bra on. She was a masterpiece, her skin told of her history and I was completely in awe. I was made for her, I am and will always be a slave to her every need and desire.

"Mark…you know this whole tough exterior thing doesn't match that soft heart of yours…" she said into my chest.

Her hair was nicely curled when I arrived but now, it was ruffled and messy, and her cheeks were still red from our activities.

"Well, this soft heart is only for you," I said looking at her.

"And the dog," I admitted.

"Oh, shit the dog!" Bellamy shot up, put her trousers back on and let Rover back in. By that time, I had my pants back on and was doing up my trousers.

"Hey boy." I smiled, giving Rover a cuddle, receiving licks to the face…

Having sex with Bellamy was amazing. Just touching her set my skin alight. The way she fit underneath me and the way I fit in her. She had told me that she hasn't slept with anyone since her ex so I wanted to make sure that every time I made love to her, she felt it; she felt the love and desire that she's always deserved and hearing her moan my name well, nothing sounded so sweet to my ears. I think today marked a big step in our relationship. She took her top off in front of me. I know how nervous she is about her body so her being comfortable enough to take her top off is a big thing for her and it made me feel like a man.

"Shall we go?" Bellamy asked looking down at me still cuddling Rover.

"Maybe you should put a top on first," I said looking at her breasts still sitting nicely in her bra.

"Oh right, yes," she laughed and headed back into her room. God, I loved this woman.

When we arrived at Bellamy's parents, she was singing along to her country music and I felt giddy with happiness.

"What are you smiling for?" Bellamy asked, still bobbing her head to the music, pulling her truck up on the curb.

"Nothing I'm just happy," I confessed.

"You might not be after this party," Bellamy said, getting out of the car leaving the door open for Rover who followed her everywhere.

"Aunty B!" A little girl shouted from the door and ran over, jumping on Bellamy.

"Oh, my sweet girl," she replied hugging her.

"Rover has missed you," she also said giving her a big kiss on the cheek.

"Who are you?" she looked over at me with her hands on her hips.

"This is my boyfriend," she said, an instant look of panic stretched her face.

"Wait, you are my boyfriend right?" she asked looking up at me.

"Well, if that's okay with you." I smiled.

"Okay yeah, so this is my boyfriend, Mark," Bellamy grinned.

"I'm Libby." She came up to me and stuck her hand out for me to shake.

"It's very nice to meet you, Libby." I smiled, shaking her hand.

"Nobody believes you're real," she then said.

"What?" Bellamy and I said in unison.

"Mum, Dad, Uncle William, everyone, they don't think you're real. Aunty B has been single for so long and apparently, you're very good looking and probably not real," she said shrugging her shoulder.

"Okay thanks, Libby, tell nanny we are here," Bellamy said pushing Libby back through the door.

"Jesus Christ," Bellamy muttered reaching out for my hand.

"I'm very good looking," I grinned feeling extremely smug.

"Yeah well she has a crush on Elmo so…" she laughed as I shoved her shoulder.

"I'm only joking," she said, kissing me on the cheek.

"Mark." I heard Beth shout from the door.

"How are you?" she said hugging me.

"Oh, hi Bellamy, how are you, Bellamy?" I heard Bellamy mutter under her breath.

"Come on in, Mark, I want you to meet everyone." Beth pulled me into the house.

"Everyone, this is Mark, Bellamy's boyfriend," she announced in the lounge to everyone.

"So you are real." A tall man walked towards me, he was definitely a sibling as he looked just like Bellamy.

"I told you," Bellamy shouted over my shoulder.

"William." He then shook my hand.

"Right Thomas you owe me a tenner!" William shouted over to the other tall guy that was walking towards me.

"You idiots really bet money on this?" Bellamy asked.

"Shit for brains," she said as she punched William on the arm.

"Here," Thomas said handing William a tenner.

"Nice to meet you, Mark, I'm Thomas," he said, shaking my hand.

"Is he real?" I heard a shout come from the toilet.

"ALEXANDER!" Bellamy shouted.

I couldn't help but laugh.

"It's nice to meet you, I'm Sarah, Williams's wife." I shook her hand.

"I'm Alice, Bell's sister and sadly his wife." She pointed to Thomas.

"It's lovely to meet you all." I smiled.

"Isn't he handsome?" Beth came over and touched my shoulder.

"Oh God," Bellamy muttered under her breath.

"I tell you, Bellamy when your aunties see him they won't leave him alone."

"You never told me I was handsome," Thomas pointed out with a frown.

"Yes, well, you don't look like that." Beth then pointed to me.

"Okay that's enough, yes he's a beautiful man and he's mine so enough!" Bellamy argued, "When's everyone else coming?" Bellamy then asked to change the topic quickly. Everyone else? Bloody hell there are loads of them already, how many more?

An hour in and Bellamy was dragged off by her niece and nephews to go and play.

"Hey, stranger." I heard a familiar voice to my left.

"Iris." I smiled.

"How are you?" I asked.

"You know she hasn't cried in years," Iris said ignoring my question and it took me a second to take in what Iris just said.

"What do you mean?"

"Bell, she hasn't cried in years not even one tear," she said lifting her index finger.

"Really?" I was shocked.

She's so kind-hearted and sensitive there is no way she hasn't cried.

"Since she came out of the hospital, she hasn't cried," she said, shrugging her shoulders.

"She just closed down," Iris continued.

I didn't really know what to say. This information has taken me by surprise. I just looked over at her smiling and laughing with the kids. Her smile was so infectious, so bright, so beautiful. "You really love her don't you?" Iris asked.

"I really do," I admitted.

Iris smiled tapped me on the shoulder and walked off. She crept slowly behind one of the twins, Austin, I think and scared him. A loud scream escaping his mouth.

"Hey Mark, watch this." I saw Alexander walk past me with a towel in his hand twisting it tight.

"Bellamy." Alexander crept over to her, her eyes darted to the towel in his hand.

"Don't you dare!" she shouted, walking backwards.

"MUM!" Bellamy screamed. She turned around, dodged Alexander and ran towards me. "Stop it!" she yelled, moving my body in front of her for protection. Bellamy let out a loud scream as I turned around I saw William flicking her with another towel that was twisted tight.

"Never gets old." They laughed high fiving each other.

"I hate you two," Bellamy hissed.

Bellamy:

After the party we called a taxi to take us home. I curled up next to Mark in bed as Rover fell asleep on the floor, the peaceful sound of his light snores filled the air.

"Thank you for coming today," I turned to Mark.

"I've had a great day today." He looked down at me.

"I love you," he said, brushing my hair out of my face, kissing my forehead.

"I love you too." I smiled, falling asleep, next to the man I loved.

Chapter Sixteen
Mark

Bellamy agreed to stay at the pub with me last night because she had a shift there at ten.

I watched intently as she slipped into a tight black dress knowing instantly it had to come off.

"I need to get into a more comfortable dress." Bellamy moaned tugging at the black material.

"Well, how about you don't put anything back on after you take that dress off," I suggested.

"As much fun as that sounds, I really need to go," she shrugged.

My arms came to my hips as I thought of a plan.

"Okay, hear me out, Maeve has got enough staff, she won't need you for at least an hour."

"Mark Barnes, you make some valid points but it's not fair of the others."

"Just give me an hour…half an hour?" I smiled, pressing my hands together in a pleading motion.

"Have you met yourself?" she said.

"Hey listen, I just like to take my time, enjoy the moment but do not doubt my abilities. Plus, I've never heard you complain before, especially when I…"

"You're killing our time here," Bellamy interrupted as she started to pull the straps from her shoulders but I stopped her.

"That's my job," I frowned.

Her hands stopped and fell to her side, rolling her eyes. I slowly pulled her dress down and traced my lips down her neck and across her chest. I pulled the dress past her vest top, down past her thong. A low moan escaped her mouth causing my intentions to become animalistic.

"Oh God," I said under my breath.

I leaned down on my knees, my hands slowly traced her hips down to her stomach.

"Mark," Bellamy said twitching with anxiety.

"Shut up!" I ordered.

My hands cupped her round bum and I squeezed.

I love this woman with all my heart. I know and I understand her anxiety with her body but it frustrates me because I don't care, I just want her. She was so incredibly beautiful to me.

"I love you," I said, coming up off the floor.

"I love you, Mr Barnes." She smiled.

I attacked her lips with mine, she allowed me better access as my tongue slipped into her mouth. I pulled my top over my head and threw it to the floor. Bellamy's hands travelled down my shoulders, past my stomach towards my belt, her hands worked fast undoing the buckle and pulled my trousers down. I kicked my jeans off my feet, picked her up and threw her on the bed.

I hovered over her and kissed her deep and hungry.

I poured myself into her as I felt her shiver and jolt underneath me.

My heart could burst. I loved her so deeply it consumed me. I love the sound of her voice and the way she touches me.

Bellamy:

The pub was extremely busy this morning but nothing could wipe this smile off my face.

The man I loved was only upstairs. My life has changed so much since Mark came back. Sometimes I had to pinch myself that he was my boyfriend. Plus, all I could think of was the amazing sex we just had.

"Excuse me, but is Mark here?" a lady asked at the counter.

"He's here somewhere," I answered smiling at her.

"Can you fetch him?" she demanded.

Fetch him? What was I? A dog?

"I'm sorry but who are you?" I asked, smiling at this stranger.

This very pretty stranger.

"I'm Sally," she said.

"Okay and Sally, who are you?" I asked again.

"Mark's wife." She smiled.

"I'm sorry what?" I asked.

I don't think I heard that right…Did she say wife?

"I'm his W…I…F…E, wife."

I looked around to see if someone was pulling a prank on me but all I saw was Anna who was standing there as shocked as I was, with her mouth gaped open, just like mine was.

"If you'll just give me a second." I smiled and walked upstairs to Mark's room.

"Mark," I shouted walking into his room.

"Yes, my love?" he came out of the bathroom with just his boxers on.

"Put some clothes on," I said. I couldn't concentrate on him looking like this.

"Why?" he asked, walking towards me and kissing my cheek.

"Because your wife is here!" I spat out.

His face dropped and his skin slowly turned grey, "My wife?" he questioned.

"Your wife," I repeated.

I stood there watching him put on a pair of jeans and a top in a hurry.

He ran past me and down the stairs.

"What are you doing here?" Mark asked with a frown on his face.

"To see my husband." She walked over and Mark took a step back.

"What's happening?" I couldn't help but ask.

"Sweetheart just go upstairs and I'll explain this all later, please," he pleaded looking over at me.

"Sweetheart?" Sally asked, her face screwing up into a ball of disgust.

"Oh, you have got to be kidding me," she huffed looking over at me. Her eyes travelled from my head slowly to my feet.

"She isn't even your type Mark, I mean really," she laughed.

"Enough!" he shouted.

"Is she your wife?" I asked just wanting the truth.

"Technically yes," he said while his face dropped to the floor.

"Technically?" my hand went to my chest and I felt a dagger being pushed and twisted.

182

"Yes, so if you can leave. I would like to talk to my husband." Sally demanded folding her arms.

I then noticed the wedding band on her left hand and the big diamond directly on top.

She smelled like Chanel and looked like a lawyer. The deep purple colour of her dress matched perfectly with her short black hair. Her eyelashes were full, lips plump and pink, her teeth were white as paper.

"Oh my God," I said looking up at Mark who had tears in his eyes.

"Bellamy," he pleaded.

I didn't say anything, I didn't know what to say. What could I say? I stormed past Mark, took my bag, which was shoved under the bar and I left, letting the door slam behind me.

I don't remember driving home.

It didn't hit me until I turned my car off and I put the key in the lock.

An hour later, I was sitting on my sofa with a whiskey in hand. I didn't know what to do or how to feel. I was trying to playback the past year of knowing Mark and he never mentioned that he had a wife, he didn't even wear a ring. I also then thought about the lovely morning we had spent together, which led to now...

"Bellamy!" I heard Mark shout from the door.

Here we go.

I walked and opened the door to reveal a tired, stressed looking Mark.

"Please go," I said looking at him with tears in my eyes.

"Don't do this Bellamy please, let me explain." Mark walked into my apartment.

"Mark…" I couldn't even get my next words out.

"I love you," Mark said reaching out for my arm.

"No, don't you dare!" I shouted taking a step back.

"I love you," he pleaded reaching for my hand, which I snatched away.

"Did you lie to me? For months. For nearly a year? You're married, for fuck's sake. Married!" I let my tears flow.

I can't remember the last time I cried but the hurt I felt was like no other.

"I trusted you, when were you going to tell me?" I said looking at him, his eyes fell to the floor.

"You were never going to tell me," my breath caught as my tears were streaming down my cheeks.

"I would have loved you even if you would have told me the truth, I still would have loved you." I took a deep shaky breath.

"Now please leave," I begged, turning around. I didn't want to see him leave, it felt like an eternity until I heard the door close. My legs gave way as I fell to the floor and cried.

***

A week later, Alice and Iris came over for a movie night. She said she wanted to check up on me but I'm pretty sure she just wanted to get away from the kids. "Oh, baby girl," Iris said, hugging me tightly.

I've kept myself pretty distracted the past week, I've been working at the hospital nonstop, if it wasn't for Taya going to the head nurse I'd still be allowed to go in and work but no.

The head nurse has sent me home, I now have three days off to wallow in my self-pity.

Since being home, I've eaten two tubs of Rossi's ice cream, I've ordered two pizzas, went down to the corner shop and brought £40 worth of chocolate, sweets and crisp.

"How are you doing, sis?" Alice asked, pulling a chip off my top.

"At least we know you're eating," Iris said.

"All I wanted was to be loved." I cried leaning into Alice's arms.

"I have this pain in my chest and it won't go away and I can't stop crying, I can't stop," I said, shaking my head gasping for air.

"You need a drink," Iris said walking to the cupboard pulling out a bottle of whiskey and three glasses.

"I can't drink," Alice said.

"But you've had Henry," I said…then it hit me.

"Wait, you're pregnant again!" I shouted.

"Yes." She smiled.

"Holy shit," Iris said pouring the liquid from the third glass into the other two glasses.

"More for us then," she muttered.

"I just want to move on, forget about him, forget about it all. Why can't I?" I asked.

"Because," Alice sighed.

"When you love someone that much, you can't just simply '*move on*'. It's not going to be like that, not when you give your heart and body to someone. It's going to hurt like hell but I promise you, you will be okay." She wiped a tear from my face.

"I let him in, Alice, I let him in. He saw me when I was in darkness. I am an idiot."

"You're not an idiot, Bellamy, you just fell in love," Iris said with gentle voice.

"Yes, like idiots do." I sniffed.

"I quit my job at the pub." I then told them.

"Really?" Alice asked looking shocked.

"Yeah, I don't really need the money. I think I was just doing it so I could see him but now I don't want to see him," I said shrugging my shoulder.

"Good for you, what film do you want to watch?" Iris asked.

"As long as it isn't a romance I'm good."

"What about a Marvel movie, those are your favourite?"

"I'm not emotionally stable enough to deal with fit superheroes," I confessed. 20 minutes later we finally decided on 'Texas Chainsaw Massacre'. Fantastic, no love, no fit celebrities, just a serial killer. Perfect.

Sitting there watching the movie, it had finally hit me. I'm not the girl that gets the guy at the end of the movie. I'm not the main character. I had this all wrong but now I understand. I'm the girl that sometimes you admire, but never the main character because that's not my story. I'm the slightly overweight girl that you won't fight for because you'd rather have the skinnier girl and that's okay because you know what? I fucking choose me and I'll choose me every single time.

Chapter Seventeen
Bellamy

"Bell, there's a letter for you," Iris shouted from the front door letting herself into my flat.

"And your point is?" I shouted back.

"I think you might want to read this one." I walked towards the sofa with a coffee in hand, the first thing I noticed was the Scottish stamp on the right-hand corner.

Addressed to, *My dearest Bellamy.*

"Holy shit," was the only word that came out of my mouth. I grabbed the letter and read.

To my Bellamy,
I owe you the truth so here it is,
Yes, Sally was my wife and yes I did love her.
But I did love her but I know for sure that I DO love you.
Three years ago, Sally and I were expecting our first child. We knew things weren't right between us but we thought the baby would fix things. Sally was 18 weeks when she lost the baby. It was going to be a girl. It broke my heart losing her and it took me a while to get over it. Sally took it badly as expected but she changed. She started drinking, going to work

with a water bottle filled with vodka. She started to blame me for our Child's death.

I didn't love her enough, I didn't care for her. The more alcohol she drank the more spiteful she got. She started to get physical with me, pushing me, hitting me.

The scar you found on my chest was when she threw a glass at me. I know what you're thinking. How can a man like me get hurt by a woman? I knew I had to leave her but I was scared. Another horrible night of abuse, I decided to book a month's stay in Portugal, I was running away. Then luckily my brother called and asked if I'd come to visit and I jumped at the opportunity.

I emailed my aunt asking her if I could stay with her until I got things sorted out.

I knew I couldn't stay in Scotland, not anymore. I wanted to try and make a new life for myself.

I left Sally three days before I left for Portugal, practically running out of the house.

Then everything changed. I saw this beautiful blonde lass sitting at a cafe with her friend and she changed my life. I know what I did was wrong. I should have been honest with you from the start and I will live with that mistake for the rest of my life.

I've moved back to Scotland for the time being trying to figure out what to do next. I have filed for divorce and she has finally moved out.

I am sorry.
All my love for now and forever, Mark.

Folding up the letter I handed it to Iris.

"Fuck me," Iris muttered. "He loves you," she continued.

"Yeah, he does," I laughed.

"What are we going to do?" Iris said with a massive smile crossing her face.

"I believe we're going to Scotland," I said standing up in my underwear and a baggy jumper.

Looking down at my appearance…

"Ah, let me get changed first."

"Good idea and maybe wash your hair." She called out to me.

Yes, I definitely need to wash my hair and maybe brush my teeth.

Twelve hours later, we had finally made it on to Scottish soil.

"Iris," I muttered. Turning my head to see her dribbling on the passenger seat. "Iris!" I shouted.

"AH FUCK!" she jumped.

"We are in Scotland now please get the address up that Scott sent you."

"Here we are." She plugged her phone into my car and the directions came up on the screen.

"Another hour away." I moaned.

I love driving but Jesus Christ if I wasn't so stubborn and listened to Iris when she said we should have stopped halfway to stay the night I wouldn't be this cranky.

"He better be worth this." Iris yawned, resting her head against the seat getting ready to fall back into her slumber.

"I don't think so." I shoved her shoulder while turning on my music.

"We are going to get through this last hour together and for your information, yes, he's worth it every single second."

Two hours later, I sent Iris back to the hotel in my car telling her that Scott said they won't be long and I quote,

Don't worry Bell we were going out for a beer, we will be home by three, and it was currently 2:30.

I waited outside his house for what seemed like forever, watching the sky turn blue to black, my hope of his arrival was ending and fast. The house sat in the middle of two others, the light brick contrasted with the black windows, which didn't seem to match the bright red front door. I was sitting on his damp doorstep, looking at my watch and seeing the clock tick over to 7:00pm.

"I'm going to kill them. I'm going to kill them both," I mutter to myself. Closing my eyes thanking it wasn't too cold tonight.

I was soon woken up by a cab door open followed by a loud eruption of laughter and shouting and then...

"Bellamy?" I heard the similar Scottish voice I've been longing for.

But oh no I shoved my butterfly aside and rose immediately to my feet.

"YOU!" I shouted pointing to him getting up from his doorstep.

"Me," he said shocked, looking behind him.

"Where have you been? I got your stupid letter and then I drove all the way to bloody Scotland. I've been sitting on your doorstep for hours. I made up this whole speech about how much I love you." I took a deep breath and continued.

"I want you, just because you're you and you are the best thing that has ever happened to me and I lost you once, and I can't lose you again. I want you, all of you. You're it for me. Like it's disgusting how much I love you. I love you, Mark

Barnes, with everything I have. But now my butt is all wet, my back aches and I haven't slept properly in 24 hours and I am so mad." Mid-sentence I realised he was laughing at me. I stopped pacing and glared back at him.

"What?" I said folding my arms watching the guy of my dreams walk towards me wearing ripped black jeans, a white top and doc martens.

He placed both hands on my face and placed a gentle kiss on my lips.

He pulled away… So I took both hands and pulled him closer and slammed my lips on his as our mouths parted the best kiss known to man was created. His arms twisted around my waist and he picked me up, my legs naturally wrapped around his waist. We both parted for air, our foreheads meeting. It was silent for a while, both of us catching our breath and enjoying this moment.

We were interrupted by the boys cheering and clapping from the taxi as embarrassment filled my face Mark chuckled, "I love you," Mark confessed.

"Madly?" I questioned.

"Madly," he replied.

Epilogue
Two Years Later – Bellamy

These past two years have brought me a whole lot of love. "Good morning," Mark said through a smile, speaking of love…

"3…2…1," I whispered and overcame Rover and our new puppy, Rupert, jumping on the bed. "You had to speak." I looked over to Mark but I couldn't see him because I had two fluffy arses in my face.

Mark thought it would be a great idea to get another golden retriever six months ago when he moved out of the pub and in with me.

We are both currently saving up for a house and at the moment we can afford about five windows.

"Right, get up!" I declared pulling the duvet off my sleepy boyfriend.

"Mark!" I walked over to his side, cupped his face and gave him a gentle kiss and within a split second, I was grabbed by my waist and pulled back onto the bed. A shriek escaped my mouth as I was slammed onto the mattress.

"I'm not ready," He laughed weighing me down.

Manoeuvring out of his arms I sat on him kissing him deeply.

I loved this man with all my heart but he's not a morning person at the moment.

"We've got to be at the airport in four hours and we still have to take the pups out," I said, breaking our kiss.

"Okay, okay," he muttered, lifting himself from the bed and walking into the bathroom.

It took me a while to get over all my insecurities with Mark.

I sometimes still find it hard to get dressed in front of him. I still get funny when he hugs me from behind and wraps his arms around my tummy. I'm getting there, very slowly.

It doesn't matter how many times he calls me beautiful or sexy.

This is my own battle in my own head that I must overcome.

***

"Are you crying?" Mark asked, trying desperately not to laugh.

"No," I whispered, wiping a tear from my eye.

"I just didn't realise how hard it would be to drop the dogs off at the kennels." I sniffed.

"We are only going to be away for two weeks," Mark said kissing my forehead.

"But what if they think we aren't coming back?" I started crying again.

"They are dogs, time is different to them, trust me they'll be okay," Mark re assured me as he drove out of the kennels. I just shrugged trying to forget about their poor little faces.

My country music was blaring from the sound system as we made our way to the airport. I looked over to Mark who was humming along to the song, with his ray bans pulled over his eyes, hand on my thigh and the other on the wheel.

I don't think there was anything sexier.

"I knew you liked this song," I giggled pointing towards him.

"It's okay." He shrugged his shoulders.

"Just face the fact you like country music now," I shrugged my shoulders

"It's okay." He repeated and turned the radio up to full volume.

"You can't drown me out!" I shouted over the music.

"But I can try." He shrugged, lifting my hand up to his mouth placing a kiss on my knuckle.

"Smooth," I said as I turned the music down.

"I love you," Mark said placing his hand back on my thigh.

"Madly?" I questioned.

"Oh, Madly Miss Edmondson." He smiled looking over at me.

"I can't believe they are here already," I huffed, staring at the whole family waiting by our space with all their luggage ready to go.

"Mark!" Libby came running over and leaping on him.

"Who's the favourite now?" Mark whispered in my ear.

"Eat shit Barnes," I muttered.

Mark:

We landed in Portugal at lunchtime.

Libby was asleep leaning on me and Bellamy's newest niece Rose was asleep on her chest, I looked over and noticed Bellamy was asleep too.

"This could be your life soon," William whispered, leaning on the row of seats in front.

"I hope so," I whispered back, not wanting to wake the three beautiful females.

We've talked about kids before and even names.

Bellamy seems like the kind of woman who wants to be married first, buy a house and then tackle kids. She's so amazing with her nieces and nephews I cannot wait to see what she's like as a mum. I know I've been a husband before and nearly a father once but with Bellamy, I know it will be so different in the best way possible.

William came over and took Rose in his arms, waking Bellamy up in the process. Then Thomas picked up Libby off the seat next to me and carried her off the plane.

A couple of hours have gone by and we arrived at the villa that Bellamy told me all about. It was sitting on top of the cliff she made me walk up nearly three years ago.

"We are home," Beth said stretching her legs.

"I've missed this place," Paul said, giving Beth a kiss on the cheek.

I would have loved to have seen my parents grow old together, I am very jealous of Bellamy still having both parents. I always wonder what it would have been like to have a father if I didn't have my brothers, God knows where I would have ended up.

The villa sat proudly in the sun. A big pool was laying at the front that was just calling for me to push Bellamy in later.

Everything was white except for the orange roof.

It was breath-taking. There were bright pink and red roses lining the driveway. It was a huge villa which slept 20 people.

I looked at my watch and noticed the time…nearly 3 o'clock. I had a lot to get done and I needed everyone's help.

Bellamy:

I slipped on my Levi shorts that I've had for three years now, a white shirt that I knotted at the front and for the first time in a long time, I just walked past the mirror.

I kissed Mark goodbye as me, Mum, Alice, Sarah and the kids went down to the shops to get stuff for breakfast in the morning. We also had to book a table at Pablo's for our first night and then I'm going to drag everyone to Alexandro's tomorrow night as Mark and I cannot wait to go back.

We soon arrived back at the villa and everything was quiet, suspiciously quiet.

I do not trust these boys, even more now they were all left on their own for an hour.

Mark fit into the family so well, it was like he's always been here. William, Alexander and Thomas called him 'Brother', Libby, Henry, Austin and Liam even came up to me and asked when they could call him Uncle Mark.

"We are back!" I shouted up the stairs, fanning my face with my hand.

"Where are the boys?" I asked Alice.

She shrugged.

"Sarah, where are the boys?" I asked as Alice wasn't giving me an answer.

"I have no idea, maybe upstairs somewhere," she said, cradling little Rose. What is up with everyone?

I made my way up the stairs until I heard something…

"Mark?" I said looking into the other rooms down the hall to find them all empty stopping when I came to our room.

I pressed my ear to the closed door.

Why was sweetheart playing by Thomas Rhett?

My ear came off the door and I twisted the knob.

"Oh, my." All I could see were tea lights and rose petals leading to the balcony. I slowly walked into the room noticing a giggle behind me.

I turned around to see everyone standing by the door.

My parents stood there proudly.

Alice and Sarah stood there with tears in their eyes and William, Alexander and Thomas, all had massive grins on their faces. The kids were just standing there, clueless about what was happening.

"Oh my God." My eyes started to tear up as I walked towards the balcony to reveal Mark standing in a suit with a huge smile on his face. The sun has not fully set so the sky was painted in a ray of warm colours.

"Mark Barnes." I smiled and walked up to him.

"Bellamy Kate Edmondson, I love you with every single inch of my heart. You are my best friend. You show me every day what true love and respect looks and feels like." Mark stopped and wiped a tear away from his face.

"I want it to be me and you, us together at the end of every day. I want to be able to hold you in 50 years and say we made it and we are still so madly in love as we watch our grandchildren play." His hand went into his pocket and pulled out a box.

"Oh my God," I whispered.

"Bellamy." Mark lowered to his knee and opened the little black box. "Will you marry me?"

"You want to marry me?" I cried, placing my hands on my heart.

"Of course I love you." Mark smiled up at me.

"I love you too, madly, Mr Barnes." I smiled through my tears.

"So…" he urged.

"Yes, yes sorry, of course, I'll marry you." I smiled leaning down to meet Mark and kissing him softly.

This feeling in my stomach was nothing but pure happiness.

I'm going to marry my best friend and my family are here in our favourite place. "This is the best day of my life." Mark smiled, pulling me up with him, slipping a beautiful, delicate ring on my finger.

All I could think to myself was…you wait till tomorrow when I tell you I'm pregnant.